Titles by *Langaa RPCIG*

Foot Prints of Destiny

Azanwi Nchami

Langaa Research & Publishing CIG
Mankon, Bamenda

Publisher:
Langaa RPCIG
Langaa Research & Publishing Common Initiative
Group
P.O. Box 902 Mankon
Bamenda
North West Region
Cameroon
Langaagrp@gmail.com
www.langaa-rpcig.net

Distributed outside N. America by African Books
Collective
orders@africanbookscollective.com
www.africanbookscollective.com

Distributed in N. America by Michigan State University Press
msupress@msu.edu
www.msupress.msu.edu

ISBN: 9956-558-83-4

DISCLAIMER

Contents

Chapter One

s his wife continued to rant and rave at his side, Paul Samba turned and gave her a resounding slap that sent her sprawling in the drying mud, 'For the last time Ekodi, I am telling you. This child is being taken to Kribi so that he might make something of himself.'

'Which other father here have you seen taking his son away to put in school?' Challenged Ekodi, fallen but not defeated.

Her husband pointed an accusing finger at her. 'You may be satisfied with the miserable life you're leading here but I'm not, Martin-Paul is going to go to school. He's going to be somebody. He won't end up a labourer like his father.'

'If you're a labourer today it is by your own choice.' his wife pointed out through her tears. 'You could have stayed in Ebolowa and farmed like your father and my father and everybody else's father has done from time ever-lasting. But no, you wanted to walk among white men and make a fortune. Whom are you blaming now for your situation?'

Paul Samba decided that it was futile trying to make his wife see his ambition as anything other than senseless. He left her whimpering on the ground and entered their hut to find out whether his son and sister-in-law were ready. Seventeen year-old Katie came out of the back room with Martin-Paul at her side. In her arms she carried little Nadja, Ekodi and Paul's other child.

'Everything ready?' asked Paul.

Katie nodded. She pointed to the small bundle standing on the table, 'Martin-Paul, you take our things and come and embrace your mother before we start off.'

1

Ekodi was slightly comforted by the fact that her sister, Katie, was accompanying her husband and her son.

She met them as they filed out of the house: 'Katie, Martin-Paul is in your hands. If anything happens to him, it's you I shall blame.'

Katie handed over little Nadja to Ekodi and hugged both of them.

'Don't worry Sis, you know I shall guard him with my life. Haven't I always done so?'

Ekodi squeezed her sister tightly to her bosom, 'You're a good girl Katie. You know the importance of family.' Then she knelt down in front of the ten year-old Martin-Paul who held little Nadja in a close hug for a moment before relinquishing her to their father.

Ekodi then held her son to her breast, the tears streaming down her face. 'You be a good boy and do everything your aunt tells you, you hear?'

Martin-Paul nodded.

'And I want you to make your father proud of you. Don't let him down, you hear me?'

Again the child nodded.

Ekodi stood up and faced her husband. They looked into each other's eyes for a minute, a secret smile on each other's lips. Then Ekodi ran into his arms. They hugged wordlessly. Ekodi dried her eyes and took the baby from him.

'I shall come for you and the baby as soon as we've found something,' Paul promised.

His wife nodded. She stood and waved until they had disappeared from her view.

They had travelled for three days, stopping each sundown at a village to ask for shelter at the home of some kind villager who was never difficult to come by. At the end of this third day, there was no village in sight and Paul Samba decided that they should camp for the night by a little stream. After a meal of roasted cocoyams and some dried meat which they had brought with them from their last place of rest, the three weary travellers fell into a deep well-earned sleep from which they did not awaken until late the next morning.

Katie was the first to wake up. Taking care not to disturb her brother-in-law and his son, she hurried to the stream for a much-needed bath (none of them had been tempted to enter the brook the night before, so exhausted had they been). The young girl scrubbed herself clean with coarse palm oil soap and a sponge of straw, then played around in the water swimming from one bank of the shallow stream to the other.

As she rose out of the water to get dressed once more, she saw a white man looking at her from under the shade of an aged Buma tree. Disconcerted, Katie was on the point of returning into the water to hide her nakedness when she decided that it would be more dignified for her to continue her walk to the bank, in spite of the stranger's eyes on her body. So she threw back her head and waded to the edge of the stream with as much stillness as she could muster under the circumstances. After she had covered her nakedness with a loincloth, securing it across her breasts, she shook Paul and Martin-Paul awake. Without saying a word she nodded in the direction of the white man, then she picked up her dirty clothes from the night before and sat down at the river bank to wash them.

The newcomer waited until both Martin-Paul and his father had washed before approaching them. The two of them also dressed in loincloths while Katie took their travelling clothes to the stream.

The white man held out a hand in greeting, 'My name is von Morgen, Kurt von Morgen. How do you do?' he said in heavily accented English.

Paul Samba took the proffered hand respectfully in both of his and introduced himself.

3

'This is your son, ja?' enquired the German.

'Yes, Massa. His name is Martin-Paul. 1 am taking him to Kribi to put him into a school there.'

'And your wife?' continued the stranger, indicating Katie who was now spreading out the washing to dry.

Paul Samba grinned at the man, 'No Massa. That's Katie, my wife's sister. She's coming to Kribi with me to keep house for me and help take care of my son.'

'Ja, ja?' nodded von Morgen as he watched Katie coming to join them, her duties completed.

'So you're all going to Kribi' said von Morgen. 'I'm going to Kribi too. You've not had breakfast as I can see. Why don't you come with me to my camp and have breakfast while you wait for your clothes to dry, ja?'

Paul Samba could not believe his ears. A white man inviting him for breakfast! He did not wait to be asked twice, but marched his family off before him, the German leading the way to his camp, which was only a few hundred yards away from theirs.

Von Morgen was not young. Neither was he old, in spite of the impressive pepper and salt beard which he affected. Of medium height and slight of build, Paul judged him to be about forty years old. He had merry blue eyes and dark brown hair streaked with grey. His voice seemed to rise out of a deep barrel.

It did not take them five minutes to reach his camp where they saw he had planted a tent. A fire was burning in front of the tent and two black men, whom Paul took to be either guides or carriers, were in the process of preparing the morning's meal.

'We have company' boomed von Morgen as soon as the two men saw him.

The German introduced his two assistants, Musi and Dinga, two young men from Bali who were his constant companions in all his travels in Kamerun.

'Massa, you travel a lot?' asked Paul Samba.

'Ja, ja,' agreed von Morgen. 'I am an explorer.' Seeing that his interlocutor had not seized the meaning of his occupation he elaborated, 'travel all over Kamerun, Ja?'

Paul nodded.

'I discover mountains, I discover rivers, villages I discover.'

Again Paul nodded, even though he was not certain he understood what the European meant by 'I discover.'

Breakfast was now ready and their host herded them to the base of a tree where Dinga had laid out bowls of steaming cereal, biscuits, canned fish, beans and hot mugs of tea.

The travellers ate with relish, to the delight of their host. Von Morgen offered Katie a second cup of tea but the girl refused with a shake of the head.

'You like tea, Ja?' enquired the German.

Katie smiled and shook her head.

At the German's look of incomprehension Paul explained. 'She does not understand English, Massa. She has lived all her life in the village.'

'Ja, ja,' exclaimed the explorer in understanding. Then he patted the young girl's hand, 'Don't worry. I'll teach you English and German,

ja?'

Katie smiled, shook her head, then said, 'ja?'

The whole company choked over their tea with laughter.

By the time the travellers reached Kribi, Paul Samba and Kurt von Morgen had become the best of friends. It was also obvious to anyone who had eyes to see that the wiry explorer was besotted by little Katie. Paul was exultant at the vista that this situation opened up to him. He made sure he described the horrors of his miserable life to the sympathetic von Morgen, sketching his ambitions for his only son and the hurdles he would have to overcome if his dreams were to be realised.

'I desire nothing for myself,' said Paul Samba with exemplary self-abnegation. 'If the doors would only open for my son, I should consider myself more than well-repaid for my efforts.'

Von Morgen, the explorer, was over and above all else a business man. He understood, with a rapidity that could only do him credit in his new friend's eyes, that what Samba needed was money.

At Kribi they parted ways, but not before the explorer had assured the labourer that he would keep in touch. He kissed Katie's hand, gave little Martin-Paul a coin.

'Goodbye, Massa Kurt.' sang both Katie and her nephew to show the progress they had made in learning the English language within the short space of three days.

Paul Samba took his family to his abode, a small two-room shack lost among hundreds of others that the Germans had had the labourers construct for their habitation - rows upon rows of identical rectangles filled to bursting with humanity. Naked children cavorted in cake mud while their mothers, in between their myriad of duties, screamed at them and laughed with each other. Each family cooked its meal in the open air behind its home, which meant that the front of your shack was the scene of your neighbour's cooking. There was one toilet and one bathroom to each row of houses, complete with shower and running water. The houses were cement-floored and brick-walled, the roofs of corrugated iron sheets.

The Africans loved it, were proud of it. This was progress, this was civilization.

Paul Samba hated it. He had not left his plot of land in Ebolowa to come and live like an ant among other ants on an anthill. There were other Africans in Kribi and elsewhere in Kamerun living like the white man, or almost - businessmen, traders, mission workers, houseboys, some royalty (although this last was a case apart) - and Paul wanted a slice of that life. The day of their arrival, before retiring for the night, he called Katie and spoke to her seriously.

'Whatever it is you're doing continue doing it. That white man, Massa Kurt, is crazy over you. Play your cards well and let yourself be guided by me. You might just end up making our fortune for us.'

Katie was a dutiful child; she was game, and it was not unflattering to have the white man so interested in her.

Her brother-in-law painted a vista of glory for her that left her panting. 'There's nothing a white man will not do for the woman he loves. You shall have everything your young heart desires - clothes, jewellery, money, European food even better than what you tasted when we met Massa Kurt on the road.'

Katie's mouth watered.

'You'd love that, wouldn't you?' asked Paul. 'Only you must not blow your chance. Before you say anything to Massa Kurt, he must come and see me. I am your lawful guardian. No man can ask for your hand without talking to me first, right?'

Samba was right.

'You'll make your sister so proud of you.' he concluded.

For five months, however, they saw no sign of von Morgen. Meanwhile, young Martin-Paul was enrolled in the small Roman Catholic school of St Augustine run by Spanish Jesuits from the island of Fernando Po. One afternoon, as the boy was returning home from school, he was met by Dinga, von Morgen's servant. Dinga handed Martin-Paul a parcel for Katie.

'Tell her it's from Massa Kurt' instructed the servant.

Katie took the parcel and kept it unopened until her brother-in-law returned from his construction work that evening. When he saw the parcel, Paul Samba smiled in satisfaction and told Katie to leave it unopened.

'The fish is beginning to smell the bait,' he exulted. That same evening Samba and his son went to von Morgen's house by the sea. Paul hid himself some distance away from the building and sent Martin-Paul with the parcel.

Von Morgen himself opened the door at Martin-Paul's knock.

'Ah, My young friend from Ebolowa,' said the German by way of greeting. 'How's school?'

'Good evening, sir,' said Martin-Paul very correctly. He held out the parcel.

'What's that, eh?' boomed von Morgen.

'Dinga sent it to my aunt this morning. She has asked me to bring it back.'

'Ja, ja? Dinga sent your auntie Katie a present?' asked the German feigning ignorance. 'What? she does not like Dinga's present?'

'She asked me to bring it back, sir,' repeated the boy.

'Ja, ja. Okay you hand the present to me, I will see that Dinga gets it, ja?'

He seized the packet from Martin-Paul's hands and examined it to see if it had been opened. Disappointed at his findings, he nevertheless drew a coin from out of his pocket and threw it to the retreating boy.

A week later, Katie received a visit from Dinga while she was alone.

'Massa Kurt has invited you for lunch on Sunday,' the Bali man informed her.

'Oh!' rejoiced Katie. 'I'm sure my moyo and his son will be happy to accept the invitation.'

'The invitation is for you alone.' specified Dinga.

Katie opened wide innocent eyes, 'Alone? You must be mistaken. Massa Kurt knows he cannot invite me without asking my guardian too.'

Dinga stood undecided what to do.

Katie came to his rescue, 'Tell Massa Kurt if he wants to see me alone, he must first talk to my moyo. If Paul tells me to come, why, I shall be only too glad to do so.''But.' Katie threw up her hands in a gesture of helplessness. 'The decision is not mine to make.'

Later that night, Dinga was back. The invitation was given to Paul Samba alone and was accepted with alacrity.

Kurt von Morgen lived in a little cottage at the edge of the sea. It was an unpretentious house some distance away from its neighbours and was surrounded by a thick hedge of bougainvilleas, orange, purple and white.

Paul Samba sat facing the German explorer across the veranda table, a glass of red wine before him. Throughout lunch they had admired the blue sea and white sands at their feet, enjoying the cool breeze that blew in from the ocean while von Morgen entertained his guest with stones about his six years so far in Kamerun. The dishes and cutlery from their meal had now been cleared by Musi. The time had come to talk business.

'How's Katie?' von Morgen enquired.

'She's doing fine, Massa.- Both she and my son send you their warm greetings.'

'Ah, yes, the young student. He's studying hard, ja?'

'I cannot complain, Massa. Last term he came first in his class. The teachers have nothing but praise for him.'

'Very good, very good.' Von Morgen cleared his throat. 'Well, my friend, I know that you need help. I have sent for you today because I think I can do something for you and your family."

Samba continued to look at the German respectfully.

'You are interested in trading, ja?' At Samba's nod the white man went on, 'This is my proposal. I can help you build a stall in the market and give you goods to stock up the place. I will also buy you a piece of land, build a house for you and your family.'

9

Samba could not believe his ears. His dreams coming true all in one day!

'In return for all this,' the German was still talking. 'You know what I want, ja?'

'Massa,' Paul Samba's voice almost choked with emotion. 'I don't know how to start thanking you.'

'Katie means a lot to me.' prodded von Morgen.

'And you shall not be disappointed.' said Paul. 'She's pure and untouched. Dutiful and obedient on top of all that. No, Massa, you can rest assured on that point. You could not have made a better choice. As soon as we have settled everything between us, I shall bring her here myself and hand her over to you.'

'But attention, ja?' went on von Morgen. 'This is all you get from me. Your business will be in your hands. If it fails I have nothing to say. Understood?'

A crafty smile stole into Samba's face, 'Don't worry Massa. This is all I need and I shall never ask for help again.'

'Just make sure you understand the terms of our deal, ja?' warned the German.

And so the Samba fortune was made, thanks to little Katie and the astuteness of the family patriarch, Paul Samba. The seventeen year-old Katie had been his charge to dispose of as he judged most profitable. He could have sold her off to some colleague of his for a few German marks, a goat and some palm wine in the name of marriage. But of what use would that have been to the family?

Katie herself was happy to be of such service to her nearest and dearest. She revelled in her new status of the white man's woman and family breadwinner. She was all that von Morgen desired and he adored her, dressing her in European finery and teaching her the mannerisms of European ladies.

As for Paul Samba, he was as good as his word and never asked von Morgen for pecuniary assistance once the white man had set him up. Starting out with a small market stall full of cotton fabrics from Europe, Samba doubled and redoubled his capital until by his third year in business, he possessed the largest market stall in Kribi. Upon von Morgen's suggestion, the now-prosperous trader built himself a large store and graduated from retailing to wholesaling, thanks to the connections he was able to make through his German friend.

Samba built a sumptuous residence on his homestead in Ebolowa and became the most influential personality in his native village, gaining even more power than the traditional chief. He was instrumental in the establishment of German rule among his people, the Bulu, when the German Protectorate of Kamerun was set up in 1884. Although this earned him the animosity of die-hard Bulu traditionalists, his affluence won him the support of large groups of coastal Bulus who subscribed to his propaganda of African advancement through European patronage.

In 1885, tragedy struck the Samba family. First of all, Katie, pregnant with von Morgen's child, died in childbirth, the baby failing to survive its mother. Then in July of that same year, embittered Bulu royalists from Ebolowa plotted the murder of Paul Samba who was suspected of having designs on the Ebolowa throne.

The bereaved and disconsolate von Morgen, threatened by the enemies of his murdered friend, decided to return to his country. But before he left, he felt there was one last favour he could do the Samba family. He went to see Paul Samba's widow in Ebolowa.

'Madam Samba' von Morgen addressed the mourning Ekodi. 'I have come to see you about something that I believe your respected husband would have wished me to do for him had he not been struck down in this tragic manner.'

At this reference to her husband's death, Ekodi's tears welled up uncontrollably.

Von Morgen continued, 'Your late husband wanted above all things to see his son not only a rich man but an educated one as well.' Ekodi nodded, unable to speak.

'I have decided to return to Germany. I would like to take Martin-Paul with me to complete his education there. His father would have eventually sent him to Europe. Also at this time, I fee! that the atmosphere here is too hostile for your son's safety. With your permission, I will take him away for some years and give his enemies v time to cool their hatred.'

Ekodi sat silently weeping for a minute, her eyes down-cast. Then she dried her tears and looked at the German. 'You're right, Massa Kurt. The boy would be safer out of the country for some time.'

She sent her six year-old daughter who was standing by her side, 'Go and fetch your brother.'

Von Morgen had one more thing to say. 'I am leaving my two houses in Kribi to your son. Until he comes back, you shall receive all the rents. There shall be no problem - I shall arrange everything with the government so that you get all the payments.'

'You have been too good to us, Massa Kurt,' wept Ekodi. 'It is nothing. Those are houses I had intended to give to Katie' here the poor man's voice broke. 'But now that she too has gone, I leave it to your son whom she loved so much.'

Martin-Paul now entered with his sister. A tall handsome boy of fifteen, he moved with a grace and talked in a gentle voice that belied the 'strength in his powerfully-built frame. He was his mother's pride and his sister's idol. Shaken to the marrow by his father's violent death, he nevertheless kept his grief in check, throwing all his energy into supervising the household and comforting his mother. Throughout all the weeping and gnashing of teeth, he had said only one thing to his mother: "I shall make all those people pay for what they have done.'

'Martin-Paul' said his mother after the boy had shaken hands with von Morgen. 'Massa Kurt is going back to his country. He wants to take you with him.'

The young man placed a hand on his mother's shoulder, 'Leave you Mama? How can I do such a thing?' He turned to von Morgen. 'I would have loved to go with you, sir. But I cannot leave my mother alone at a time like this.'

'I am not leaving immediately, young man.' said von Morgen. 'It will take me another two months to wind up things here.'

'We must not neglect your education, my son' said Ekodi.

'You know your father had ambitions for you. You would be doing him a great disrespect to pass over this chance of furthering your studies overseas. And I shan't be alone. Your father's brothers will be here to take care of me till you come back.'

Martin-Paul stared at his feet, lost in thought.

Ekodi got up and passed an arm round his shoulders. 'My son, we believe it is better that you leave the country for some time.'

Martin-Paul was still staring at his feet. When he looked up after a minute his face had cleared. 'Very well, I shall go. But,' he turned to von Morgen. 'You must promise me one thing.'

'What?'

'That I shall enter a military school. I want to be a soldier.'

Von Morgen gave him a broad grin, 'That is no problem, my boy. The German Government is looking for young men like you to train for their overseas services. When you come back to Kamerun, you can be assured of a high and privileged position in the army.'

As the carriage rolled away from Ulm train station that afternoon, Martin-Paul eyed his companion curiously. Von Morgen seemed to have become progressively taciturn as their journey neared its end. The boy drew his overcoat tighter around his shoulders. God, it was cold! He re-arranged the heavy rug covering his knees and legs.

The German gave him a bleak smile, 'You're cold, ja?'

Martin-Paul grinned wryly, 'This is quite different from Kribi.'

'You'll get used to it.'

The usually jovial German looked downright depressed. Martin-Paul could not begin to imagine why. Surely the man should be excited to be returning home again after such a long absence. For his part, the boy, though chilled to the bone, was elated to find himself in the white man's country. Germany was all that he had imagined and more. The long train journey from Hamburg to Ulm had been tiring but also exhilarat-ing. Only the obvious sadness of his friend had prevented him from exclaiming out loud at the sights - the huge buildings, the streets of Hamburg, the crowds, the carriages, the elegantly dressed men and women (for now the boy was not seeing the poor and miserable), everything he saw filled him with wonder and admiration. The contrast between this and what he was used to in Africa left him shaking his head in amazement.

Then they were there. Through the glass window of the carriage, Martin-Paul saw they "were driving up to an impressive mansion, two stories high and built of darkened red brick. On either side of the driveway, a wide expanse of smooth lawn broken only by flower-beds and fountains stretched into woods.

The vehicle drew up before wide frontsteps. Martin-Paul looked at von Morgen expectantly.

'We're home,' said the German laconically.

The driver had the door open and was placing portable wooden steps at the carriage entrance. Martin-Paul allowed his companion to descend first. The front door opened and an elderly woman came down to meet them. She embraced von Morgen with tears in her eyes.

14

'It's so good to see you, Brother!' she exclaimed.

Von Morgen returned her hug absently and introduced her to Martin-Paul, 'My sister, Myra.'

The woman welcomed the boy warmly albeit with a look of surprise.

'What do they call you dear?' she enquired in a motherly tone.

'Martin-Paul, Ma'am.' Coming from the Kamerun coast, Martin-Paul could hold his own in the German tongue. He had moreover been polishing up on the language during the past several months in anticipation of his arrival in Germany.

The driver started carrying their luggage into the house aided by another servant who had come out of the house and whom the woman had introduced to von Morgen as the new servant, Fritz.

'How is the family, Myra?' enquired von Morgen as his sister stood looking at him undecidedly.

'Oh, Brother,' exclaimed Myra as if she had been waiting for this cue. Her eyes welled up once more. 'It is so lucky that you have at last come back. I have been at my wits' end.'

Von Morgen stiffened, 'Sonia?'

'And Maria. I don't know who is worse. Really I don't know.' Myra wrung her hands in distress, her eyes brimming.

'What has happened?' bellowed von Morgen seeming to emerge from his apathy for the first time.

The front door was noisily flung wide open and they all looked up. A girl stood on the top step and returned their look with an insolent stare before descending the steps. The three people by the carnage watched as she seemed to glide towards them, her long skirts floating behind her. Martin-Paul was fascinated. The girl had abundant yellow hair tied back m a ponytail that fell to her hips. Her eyes were blue-no, green-no, blue-green, like the colour of the sea at Kribi on a windy day. And her hair wasn't yellow, it was more the

colour of the white sands of Kribi beach. She had full wide
lips the colour of - of ripe guava pulp. It was hard to tell
but as she drew closer, Martin-Paul saw she was younger
than he had first imagined her to be - probably about his
own age.

The girl went straight to von Morgen and held out her
hand, 'Welcome back.'

The explorer drew her to him and hugged her
unresponding body, 'Sonia, my dear, aren't you happy to
see me?'

The girl favoured him with a quizzical smile and turned
to Martin-Paul, 'Who is that?'

Von Morgen took her hand and introduced Martin-Paul.
'This' he told the boy, 'is my daughter, Sonia'

Martin-Paul gaped. Von Morgen had a child and had never
even hinted at it!

Sonia shook hands with her father's protégé, her frank
gaze examin-ing him minutely. She noticed he was trying
rather unsuccessfully to keep his teeth from chattering. 'Why,
he's cold, Papa!' she exclaimed. 'You poor thing! I hear it's
hotter than hell in Africa. Is that true?'

Martin-Paul smiled and nodded.

'But let's go in first before you freeze!' she led the way
still talking, 'Though I don't know what you're going to do
in winter. This is only September.

'In two months the snow will be here.' She looked at
Martin-Paul with laughter-filled eyes. 'Wonder what you're
going to do then? It's going to get much, much colder, you
know.'

Martin-Paul looked gravely back at her, 'If it gets too
cold for me, I'll fly back home on the wings of a migrating
bird.'

Sonia threw back her head and laughed throatily. She
had a deep voice that she had obviously inherited from her
father.

She slipped her hand into Martin-Paul's, 'I think I'm going to like you. I don't like many people, you know. I don't even like my father.'

Martin-Paul heard a quick intake of breath behind him as Sonia opened a door and they entered the drawing room where a lively fire was blazing. He stole a look at von Morgen to see what effect his daughter's words had had on him. The explorer had a vacant look in his eyes.

While everybody found a seat for themselves, Martin-Paul made a beeline for the fireplace and sat down cross-legged on the soft grey carpet, as close to the fire as possible, stretching his hands out to the flames. A maid came in with a tray of refreshments - tea, buns and scones. Sonia poured out a cup for everybody.

'You haven't asked for Mama, Papa' she commented as she handed her father a cup.

'Where is she?' demanded von Morgen.

Sonia sat down before answering, 'We'll go up to her after we've had something to eat. She isn't feeling well.'

They sat eating in silence while Martin-Paul admired the vast room they were in. Autumn sunlight poured through the spotless window-panes. There was a grand piano at one end of the room, between a round glass window and a door which led to a side veranda. A few beautiful paintings hung in gold frames on the walls. Martin-Paul felt the blood beginning to circulate again in his veins from the combined warmth of the tea and the drawing-room fire. He was the only one eating with an appetite. Von Morgen drank two cups of tea and sat looking out the window nearest to him. Myra took a couple of sips and tore a scone to shreds in her saucer. Sonia sat drumming on the armrests of her seat and watched her father with intense eyes.

As soon as Martin-Paul was finished, the girl sprang up, 'well, shall we all go up and say hello to the lady of the house?'

They trooped out of the living-room, Sonia leading, Martin-Paul and Myra bringing up the rear. On the first floor they turned right and entered a dim but large bedroom with a canopied bed. Sonia ran to draw back the heavy curtains by the bed so that the occupant of the bed could be clearly seen. She was propped up to a seating position with several pillows against the head of the bed. Von Morgen stood before her and stared for a full minute. Then he sank down on his knees and buried his face in his hands.

The woman on the bed looked like one of the many jujus that used to frighten Martin-Paul as a child growing up in Ebolowa. Only the face Martin-Paul was looking at now was no painted wooden mask but flesh and blood, hard as it was to believe it. Her head was completely bald, shining whitely like a dome. One side of her face was swollen while the other half was bony, the cheek sunken, twisting her mouth away from the centre of the grotesque face. The woman wore an outsized lacy nightdress out of which stuck a think stick-like right arm, the birdlike fingers clawing restlessly on the rich red counter-pane. The left arm, like the left cheek, was swollen out of all proportion, the fingers looking more like sausages than anything human. The swollen arm and fingers lay inert supported by a sling hung round the sick woman's neck.

The woman spoke, looking down at the kneeling figure of her husband. 'So you've come back in time to see me before I die, Kurt von Morgen.' Her voice was hoarse and scarcely audible. The displacement of her mouth made her pronunciation difficult and it was only by straining the ear that meaning could be made out of her mumble.

Von Morgen reached out a hand to touch her but stopped halfway as if in fear. The ghostly right hand was clawing at the counterpane while the woman moaned softly with each breath.

'Maria,' groaned von Morgen. 'What in Heaven's name happened to you?'

The woman moaned louder in her effort to speak. Martin-Paul looked away unable to stand her obvious suffering.

'I got cancer, Kurt.' Her voice seemed to be reaching Martin-Paul from the other side of the grave. 'I have been operated on eight times in the last four years.'

Martin-Paul looked over at Sonia but she was standing at the window her back to the room. It seemed impossible to the boy that this caricature in the bed was her mother. What kind of illness was this that could change a human being into an animal? They all turned as the door opened to let in an efficient-looking nurse who bustled them out saying that her patient had had enough excitement for the day.

Martin-Paul watched von Morgen walking ahead of him with the gait of an old man - back bent feet shuffling as if held down by weights. He was fast losing any resemblance to the jaunty explorer who had wooed and won the young man's aunt not such a long time ago. Sonia came flying past him, running down the stairs and out of the house into the gathering evening. Von Morgen crossed the landing to what Martin-Paul supposed were his own apartments. The boy stood undecided at the top of the stairs. What a welcome into the country he had dreamed of visiting from the time he started going to school.

What a welcome for von Morgen who had not seen his family for six years! He decided to go down into the drawing room and await further developments since it appeared he had temporarily been forgotten.

But just then von Morgen's sister appeared in the hall - and proposed to take him to his own rooms. Martin-Paul followed her down the stairs to the lower left wing of the house where he was shown an apartment complete with bathroom and bedroom for his personal use. It was as lavishly furnished as the rest of the house and made the guest wish his friends in Africa could see it. His luggage was already waiting in his front room.

Myra went out saying, I'm sure you'll want to take a bath. I'll ask the maid to bring you some hot water.'

Martin-Paul set about unpacking. He had brought two huge suitcases of clothes and shoes, scarves, boots, handkerchiefs, hats, all bought for him in Hamburg by von Morgen. Nothing that he needed in the way of dress had been forgotten. The German would not let Martin-Paul protest over the vast sums that were being spent on him.

'Until you leave Germany you're under my care,' von Morgen had stressed. 'And anything I would do for a son, I shall do for you.'

The maid came in with two buckets of hot water and another four of cold water. As he finished putting his things away she filled the bath and stood at the bathroom door.

'Your bath is ready sir,' she informed him.

'Thank you,' he replied shutting his now empty suitcases.

'Will you need me to scrub your back, Sir?'

Martin-Paul interrupted his task to take a good look at her. She was buxom and fair, with rosy cheeks on a pretty face.

'What's your name?' the boy asked her.

'Martha, Sir.'

'Well, thank you, Martha, but I won't need you to scrub my back.' He wondered if she had been joking, but she looked at him matter-of-factly and started packing her buckets in readiness for departure. I suppose it's all part of the luxurious life here, Martin-Paul told himself.

'Oh,' he called as Martha went out, T shall need another pail of water to rinse myself with.' Luxury or not, he did not hold with washing and rinsing himself in the same bath of water - it left him feeling unclean.

Supper that night was eaten only by Myra and himself. Neither his host nor his host's daughter was in sight. The matronly Fraulem Myra ate without a word, heaving a sigh between each mouthful. At the end of the meal, von Morgen showed up. As his sister left the table, he sat down opposite his guest and apologised for his absence.

'I was taking some much-needed rest.'

Martin-Paul said he understood.

The maid, Martha, brought in some wine which von Morgen poured out for Martin-Paul and himself. The boy took a cautious sip. It was sweet and heady. He nursed it, not wanting to risk getting drunk.

Von Morgen drank thirstily and refilled his glass. 'You won't be able to start school until January when the next school year begins.' Martin-Paul nodded, 'You told me that, sir'

This is not a bad thing for you. You will be able to acquaint yourself with a lot of things and get to feel at home before that time. Can you ride?'

'Not really, sir.'

'Well, that's something you can start practising right away. We've got plenty of horses. Sonia or a groom, can give you a few lessons until you enter the Gymnasium. You know horsemanship is an important part of the school curriculum. If I were you, I should also keep up with my lessons. The academic part of the Gymnasium's program is no less important than the others. So you see, you shall have enough to keep you occupied for the next three months.'

'Oh, as for that, sir,' Martin-Paul hastened to reassure his friend.

'There can be no danger of my getting bored. You have a fabulous home and everything here is new to me. Just exploring the town and getting to know my way around will keep me busy enough.'

Von Morgen finished his second glass of wine and poured out a third.

Martin-Paul looked at the former explorer with compassion. The

German had aged since their arrival this afternoon and now looked all of his fifty-five years.

The old man returned Martin-Paul's look. 'You're surprised to discover I have a wife and daughter, ja?'

Martin-Paul chose to be diplomatic, 'It is a normal thing in life, sir. Although I'm very sorry about your wife's illness.'

'Ah, yes, Maria, my wife. The most beautiful girl East of the Rhine. It is hard to believe what illness has turned her into.'

'I know it's a heavy blow for you, sir.'

'So it is, my son, so it is. What is a beautiful face, a tempting figure? Just so much straw to be burnt by the fire of time. Maria was a beautiful woman. She is no more.'

Martin-Paul looked at von Morgen in puzzlement. What was the man trying to say? Was he sorry about his wife or what?

Although Martin-Paul was exhausted by the time he went to bed, he was not to get the rest he deserved. He woke up at one o'clock in a sweat, after dreaming that he was an eight year-old boy in Ebolowa again, with Maria von Morgen for a mother. As he sat up in bed and tried to compose himself, he heard footsteps in his parlour. Somebody was walking about in there stopping from time to time before the bedroom door. For a moment Martin-Paul's heart stood still. Could it be the sick woman from upstairs? What on earth could she want with him? Then the boy chided himself. Come on, Samba. You know that poor woman cannot leave her bed, much less walk down those stairs into your apartments. He listened at the keyhole and bet with himself that that light tread belonged to Sonia von Morgen. Samba waited until she was standing at the bedroom door again. Then as she moved on, he opened the door swiftly and caught her in his arms before she had taken two steps. She gave a small yelp of fright then stood still.

'What do you want, Sonia?' Martin-Paul asked from behind her.

She twisted round in his arms to face him, 'I'm so glad you're awake, Martin-Paul. I came to invite you up to Mama's room. You haven't really met her yet and I want her to see you.'

Samba let her go, 'What? Are you crazy? Do you know what time it is?'

'I know it's late but, you see, Mamma doesn't sleep much, neither do I. So she's glad to have a visit at any time of night or day.'

'Good Heavens!'

Sonia groped for him in the dark and touched his arm.

'What's so crazy about it? After all you were awake.'

'Only because you woke me up,' growled Samba.

'Well then, now you're awake, and you won't be able to go back to sleep right away.'

'So why not come up with me and say hello to Mama? It isn't right that she hasn't met you yet.'

Martin-Paul searched blindly for the tinder box and found it. As he struck the light, he told himself that Maria von Morgen's face was the last thing he wanted to see in the middle of the night. Nevertheless he followed Sonia to her mother's room.

Sonia stood at the head of the bed. 'Mama, I want you to meet Martin-Paul. He arrived with Papa today. His father was Papa's closest friend in Africa. He's going to enter the Gymnasium here in Ulm and become a soldier.' She beckoned for Samba to stand by her side.

Maria von Morgen lay on her back, the bedclothes covering her right up to the chin.

'Mama, are you asleep'? Sonia bent over her mother's face and listened. Then she pushed back the bedclothes hastily and placed a hand on the woman's chest.

'Ma-am-a-a!' Sonia's shriek rent the stillness of the cool autumn night.

Martin-Paul pushed the girl aside and took Maria von Morgen's wasted right wrist in his hand to feel the pulse. The door of an adjoining room opened and the nurse rushed in, almost tripping in her long voluminous nightgown.

'What, what?' croaked the woman, still groggy from sleep.

„ Sonia pushed Samba out of the way and fell on her mother's body.

'She's dead, she's dead' the girl screamed.

The nurse threw Sonia on the floor and felt the patient's pulse. Von Morgen and his sister came running in as the woman straightened up after listening for the non-existent heartbeat.

'She's gone.' Announced the nurse.

After that there was pandemonium. Fritz and Samba carried a screaming Sonia to her room opposite von Morgen's and held her there forcibly until a doctor arrived an hour later with something to send the hysterical girl to sleep.

The next day passed in a whirlwind of preparations for the funeral and visitors streaming in to exclaim at von Morgen's return and offer their sympathy. Sonia awakened only to be sent back to a drugged sleep after threatening to resume her hysterics.

By the day of the funeral she was much calmer if tearful. The Roman Catholic cathedral was packed to bursting with friends who had lived for the past year in daily expectation of Maria von Morgen's death. Samba felt the tears start to his eyes as he listened to the priest's homily. Several people cried unabashedly.

'For four years,' said the priest, 'we have watched Maria von Morgen fight a dreadful battle with death, and many of us have prayed for the Lord in His mercy to release this woman from her agony. Why then are we tearful today? Is it because we are sorry that her struggle has finally come to an end? If we are crying today it certainly is not for Maria. It is for ourselves. We have no more reason to be sorry for Maria. She is now finally at peace. Twice in the past year she received the last sacrament thinking like all of us that the end had come. Can we now doubt that she is anywhere but at out Lord's feet at this moment? No, we should not weep for Maria. This courageous woman has at last found the ultimate peace.'

Samba dried his eyes and followed the procession to the von Morgen cemetery. As the coffin was lowered, Sonia and her aunt fell weeping into each other's arms. Then the family members were asked to throw in the first handfuls of earth.

As von Morgen stepped forward to comply with the ritual, he was overcome with emotion and fell to his knees sobbing.

Immediately Sonia was standing over her father, raining abuses at him. 'Why are you pretending to be broken-hearted now?' the girl shouted for all to hear. 'Why are you shedding crocodile tears? Where were you when she needed you? Where have you been all these years when she was sick and atone?' She grabbed her kneeling father by the shoulders and shook him in fury. 'Don't come crying at .my mother's grave. She was nothing to you. Go back, go back where you came from!'

The momentarily paralysed Samba suddenly regained the use of his limbs and jumped to the girl's side just as the servant, Fritz, reached her. Together they dragged the raving Sonia away from her father and the cemetery, away from the gaping crowd of mourners.

Samba knocked on von Morgen's library door and went in. The German sat at his writing table, his back to the door, staring out through the window into the garden.

'She's sleeping at last, sir,' said the boy. 'The doctor has left something for her to be taken every day until he tells her to stop.'

Von Morgen nodded without looking round, 'Thank you, my boy.

You've turned out to be a great asset to me. I am grateful.'

T wish I could do more, sir. I am very sorry about your wife's death.'

Von Morgen turned and faced the boy. 'I think I owe you an explanation after all that has happened since my return.'

He motioned Samba to a seat beside him.

After the boy had taken the seat, he went on, 'My wife and I had a terrible quarrel many years ago when Sonia was just four years old; so terrible that I decided to leave Germany and never come back. I wanted nothing to do with the civilised world ever again. So I went to Africa, perhaps with the vague hope of meeting with death there. For there was a pain in my heart bigger than I could carry.'

'After four years, I returned to Germany. I don't know why. Maybe I wanted to see my child. Maybe I hoped that Maria and I could forget the bitter past and start anew. But when I arrived I knew I had made a mistake in coming back. My wife had not missed me. She did not need me. I left Germany even more bitter than I had been the first time, if you can imagine that.'

'Well, you know what happened to me after that. For a while, Katie brought joy into my life again. I would have spent the rest of my days in Kamerun had she not died. I had no idea that Maria had fallen sick meanwhile. The Lord will forgive me but when I saw her upon my return home, I felt she had received just payment for the hurt she had caused me, her husband. Even now, after all she has gone through, I cannot think of her without some resentment. Her death has not caused me pain - at least not much. No, if I am sad today, it is because of my daughter. I see now that I made a mistake in leaving her with her mother, for Maria has turned the child away from me. She blames me for Maria's death, and yet I cannot find it in my heart to tell her the truth about her mother. She was too young to see the truth, and now it might be too late to make her understand.'

Samba was exhausted. He had not slept for three days. By the time von Morgen came to the end of his story, the boy's head was nodding drowsily.

'Ach'! von Morgen exclaimed when he noticed. He touched Samba's knee, 'Go and get some rest, my boy, and thank you for all you've done.'

Martin-Paul stared guiltily, 'I'm sorry, sir. We must find a way of making Sonia understand. That is the only way out.'

Von Morgen smiled warmly at him 'You're a good boy, Martin-Paul. Now go to bed.'

Samba handed the drawing to Sonia. 'There! It looks something like that.'

'O-o-oh,' exclaimed the girl after glancing at the sketch. 'It looks exactly like an igloo.'

'You're right,' agreed Samba. 'The similarity never struck me before, but, it does look very much like an igloo.'

'But you don't have snow in Africa, do you?'

'No, we don't.'

'So what are the walls made of?'

'Mud.'

'I beg your pardon?'

"The walls are made of mud. Here, let me have that paper again.'

He took the paper from Sonia and drew another sketch.

'This is how it's done.' He drew his chair closer to Sonia's bed; 'See these? They are poles stuck into the ground - heavy poles. That's the first step. Then more flexible poles, bamboo poles like the ones you use in making cane chairs, only these are bigger. Well, these bamboos are tied criss-cross to the first poles to form a crude lattice-work. An opening is left for a door and one or two windows, and that's it.'

'And the mud?'

'Yes, that's the easy part. The earth is dug up and mixed with water to the right consistency. At that point, the builders just slap it onto the bamboo frame, both inside and outside, to form the walls. Simplicity itself.'

'Surely, they don't use it for the roof also. Something tells me that wouldn't work out well.'

'And you're right,' smiled Martin-Paul. 'No, the roof is covered with sheaves of palm leaves or grass, closely packed and woven together.'

'I've seen that here!' cried Sonia triumphantly, 'on farms in the countryside. Most barns are built that way.'

'Are they really?' It was Samba's turn to be surprised. 'I didn't think people here built anything but brick and stone houses.'

'You'd be surprised. Just wait till I take you sightseeing around the village.'

'I can't wait. I'm too impatient. How about tomorrow?'

'Right, bright and early. Can you ride?'

'Not really, but I'm anxious to learn.'

'I'll be your teacher, I know just the horse for you.'

Samba's heart was singing. For the first time since her mother's death a month ago, Sonia had accepted to step out of the house.

Next morning she met him as he was leaving his apartment to come in search for her.

'My,' exclaimed the girl. 'Don't you look dashing! A dark knight from a fairytale castle. All that's lacking at this moment is your horse.'

Samba was dressed in expensive riding clothes and boots that von had had made for him in Hamburg. He, too, had been impressed by the figure he cut in the mirror this morning.

'You look unreal yourself, Sonia;' he said, returning her compliment. It was the first time he was seeing a woman in men's clothing. The effect on him was rather overwhelming.

'Oh, everybody disapproves of my riding tenue,' said Sonia airily, 'but I just can't stand riding in a dress. Mama had them make this one specially for me.'

'Every time I wear it I get a strange feeling of power and freedom that's hard "o explain to the disapproving ladies of this village.'

'I like it,' said Samba sincerely. 'Very much.' He could see her point.' What fun could there be, riding in a dress ?

28

Their friendship grew with each passing day. Samba was determined that the girl should not sink back into the depression that had almost brought her to the brink of insanity. He felt as if he was in a constant tussle with the devil himself for Sonia's soul. Of the entire von Morgen household the African was the only person the girl could open up to. She didn't even want to see her father and von Morgen, wisely, stayed out of her way.

She loved to hear about Africa and Samba had an inexhaustible fund of information about this fascinating continent to keep him talking for even longer than Scheherazade's *thousand and one nights.* There were several nights when the girl could not find sleep. She would come knocking on Samba's door in the middle of the night and beg him to let her sleep in his bed. She would talk incoherently of menacing little men invading her room from the roof and walls. 'They're just waiting for me to go to sleep so they can jump on me and cut off my .head!' she would weep. Samba would take her to his bed and wrap his arms comfortingly around her until she fell asleep. Next morning she would appear to have forgotten all about her hallucinations. Samba himself was mystified but decided to keep his knowledge of these episodes to himself.

One day Sonia took Samba to the von Morgen picture gallery, a long room built beneath the ground floor of the mansion. There," for the first time, the boy saw a likeness of the late Maria von Morgen. He stood transfixed before the portrait of the young maiden who looked so much like Sonia, yet more ethereal. It was hard to reconcile these feature with those of the suffering crone he had seen the day he arrived at Ulm.

'She was lovely wasn't she?' asked Sonia quietly beside him.

'But my father didn't love her.'

'You don't know that for sure, Sonia.'

'Don't I? How else was I supposed to interpret the fact that he abandoned her for ten years. Abandoned me too. How can I ever forget the time he came home six years ago. I begged him, I cried, I refused to eat- all in an effort to make him stay. The day he was leaving I clung to him and wouldn't let go. They had to pry him loose. But nothing could move my darling father. Neither Mama's pleas nor mine had any effect on him.'

"Did your mother also beg him to stay?'

'Of course!'

'Are you sure?'

'What kind of question is that?'

'I'm not trying to call you a liar.'

'Mama told me she begged him on her knees to stay, but it was of no use.'

A week before Christmas, an excited Martha came to Samba with a letter. She had a friend, she said, who worked at the home of a Presbyterian Pastor in Stuttgart. Happening to have come to Ulm some time ago, this friend of Martha's had mentioned the arrival at the Pastor's home of two young men from Kamerun who were supposed to enrol at the Ulm Gymnasium in the new year. Martha, who had remembered that Samba was also from Kamerun, had urged her friend to inform the Pastor's guests of Samba's presence in Ulm. The outcome had been a letter sent through Martha's friend to Martin-Paul, from his compatriots in Stuttgart.

Samba was thrilled at Martha's news and tore open his letter excitedly. It was a short note that brought a smile to the reader's face.

If you are the person we think you are, then know that your late father was a great friend of ours. The great Paul Samba was closely associated in business with our family.

We hear you are also headed for the famous Gymnasium for studies. We look forward to seeing you there on the first day of term. You shall be able to recognize yours truly by the hat I shall be wearing. I need not say more.

Before I say goodbye permit us to introduce ourselves as Felix Ndolo Bele and the one and only.

Rudolph Ndumbe Douala Manga Bell

Samba finished the letter and gave the watching Martha a grateful hug. Then he took the stairs two at a time and stood knocking at Sonia's door.

'Oh - oh - oh,' cried Sonia collapsing on her bed after reading the note. 'This is the funniest thing I've read in ages. Who is he?'

Samba was grinning, 'I don't know him. But I do know the name. His father is paramount chief of the coastal tribe of Douala, the first people to have come in contact with Europeans in Kamerun. The Manga Bells are an important royal family in Kamerun.'

Sonia shook with laughter. 'The one and only.' She took up the letter and read, 'Rudolph Ndumbe Douala Manga Bell. Oh, I shall make sure I come with you and Papa the day you leave for the Gymnasium. I wouldn't miss seeing that hat for all the gold in Arabia!'

For the second time Samba congratulated himself. Sonia had commit-ted herself to travelling in her father's company.

After a Christmas which, because of the recent bereavement of the von Morgen family, could not have been otherwise than quiet, the entire household was plunged into the excitement of seeing Samba off to school. Martha gave him a pretty many-coloured quilt which she had started making from the first week Samba arrived at Ulm. There was a pair of mittens, a scarf and a cap to match. These, Martha informed the boy, had been made long before his arrival.

'Who for'? Samba wondered, Martha just smiled coyly, 'Maybe I knew you were coming.' Samba rewarded the maid with a bear hug and promised to remember her each time he used her presents.

Sonia gave him a big leather-bound diary, 'I want you to note down everything interesting that happens to you and tell me all about it during the holidays.'

When the big day came round, Fraulein Myra von Morgen handed him a mammoth-sized apple strudel, still hot from the oven. 'This should help break the ice between you and your friends,' said the lady.

Von Morgen gave him a fat cheque to be cashed at a bank in the city. Samba knew the German was grateful to him for the help he had been with Sonia. From flatly refusing to see her father immediately following her breakdown, Sonia was now deigning to exchange civilities with von Morgen. The trip to the city to see off Samba was a major coup which, after consultation with each other Samba and von Morgen had decided to capitalise on.

The plan was that, after saying goodbye to Samba, von Morgen would take his daughter to an inn for the night. There, after dinner and an opera or other musical, his daughter in a mellow mood, the explorer would have a heart to heart with his daughter, and try to state his own case without hurting the girl's memory of her mother. It was not going to be an easy day for von Morgen but, as Samba told the old man, if he was sincere, then the game was already half-won. With the heavy snowfall outside, the classrooms had been opened so that parents and friends could say their last goodbyes without freezing.

Samba and von Morgen followed Sonia as she dashed in and out of rooms wanting to be the first of the party to spot Rudolph Manga Bell.

'There he is!' the girl cried finally.

She had seen only the headgear but nobody had to tell her who it was. She did not think that two people on earth could have had the idea of sporting such a hat in a place like this.

The young man in question was sited cross-legged on the teacher's table holding forth to a group of fascinated youngsters around him. He saw Samba as soon as they entered the room and left his perch to meet them. Everybody made way for him to pass. He walked with long stately strides, a tall eighteen year-old fellow with very fair black skin, lips that smiled even in repose, merry eyes and a dashing manner. He was dressed expensively in well-fitting European clothes, and on his head was the hat that had everybody staring at him in puzzlement. It sat on his head like a crown but looked like a wide-rimmed basket filled with exotic coloured feathers. The plumes were so long and delicate that they swayed and swirled from side to side with each step the young man took.

He held out his hand to Samba, 'Martin-Paul Samba, I presume? I am Rudolph Manga Bell. And this,' he turned to the slim youth who had materialised at his side 'is my cousin, Felix Bele.' Felix was as light-skinned as his cousin with an angelic face. He had long-lashed brown eyes and a sunny smile. Samba shook hands with both young men and introduced Sonia and her father who had been staring fascinated at the unself-conscious Rudolph.

As soon as he noticed Sonia the young Manga Bell swept off his plume-laden hat in a courtly gesture, bowed from the waist and took the girl's proffered hand to his lips. Sonia pressed her lips tight to keep from laughing at the young prince's flamboyant manner, and turned hastily to shake hands with the Adonis at his side.

While Rudolph put his hat back on, von Morgen commented.

'I've seen that headgear before. It certainly isn't part of the Douala royal costume.'

Both Felix and the prince favoured the German with sour looks.

'How would you know that?' queried Rudolph.

'He's lived in Kamerun for the past ten years,' Samba informed his new friend.

Rudolph looked at von Morgen with more respect 'if that's the case then you must know that the Doualas have nothing to compare with this in impressiveness. It's actually the head-dress of Bamileke women dancers;' he told his friends in a lowered voice. 'But who else around here knows that? I was just telling them before you came in that these feathers have special protective powers against evil spirits.'

'Are you trying to scare everybody away from you?' asked Samba.

Rudolph smiled wisely. 'First impressions are lasting impressions. It never did anybody harm to inspire a little awe in his entourage.' Turning to Samba T might as well warn you as I've warned my cousin, I plan to play up my blue blood to its limits. So be prepared to play along with me.'

Rudolph lived up to his word. And it stood him and his friends in good stead. The first victory he won for them was to obtain permission from the head of the school for he and his two Kamerunian friends to sleep side by side in the same dormitory. As Samba told Sonia later during the holidays, the young prince spent the whole of his first week establishing his sovereignty over both students and teachers alike.

That first day, finding that Samba, Felix and himself had been assigned to different dormitories, Rudolph discarded his European apparel and donned a multi-coloured flowing robe of ample propor-tions - a garment which, Samba informed Sonia, was the traditional court dress of a northern Kamerunian tribe. With this, Rudolph put on a matching cape resembling a judge's wig in shape but gaudily embroi-dered and beaded.

'With that, he marched us off to the principal's house and boldly knocked on the door. You should have seen his wife's face when she answered the door.'

'Oh - oh - oh I can imagine it!' Soma hooted.

'Rudolph stood in the centre of the principal's living-room and delivered this speech about how he was heir apparent to the Kameru-nian throne and we were his nchindas.'

'What's that?'

'Bodyguards, if you please.'

'Oh-oh-oh.'

'He said it would be traditionally sacrilegious for him to sleep ' flanked by any persons other than his nchindas. We were going to stand outside in the snow, he said, until arrangements could be made for us to be together. Of course the principal couldn't let the Kamerunian prince freeze in the snow. He could not tell what diplomatic repercussions that might have had.'

Because of Rudolph, the 'Kamerunian contingent' as the three friends came to be nicknamed, had a much easier time of it in school than the other newcomers. They were not forced to perform menial duties for the senior students such as laundry or boot-polishing. They were never made the butt of the senior students' sadistic proclivities. First year students could be given corporal punishment by the seniors for as little a crime as failing to stand still and wait for a senior student to pass if one happened to be met in a corridor. When Rudolph Manga Bell passed, everybody made way for him.

In the refectory it was a strict law that nobody at a table served himself before the table head, who was always a senior student of course. Heads of tables often came to the refectory at the end of the dining period so that the younger students sometimes had to gobble down an insufficient amount of food and go around on a growling stomach until the next meal. Unlike the older students who could get out of the school confines and buy food, the newcomers were not allowed to leave the compound except on holidays. They were not allowed to bring in any extra food either. Exception was made for the Kamerunian contingent of course. From the first week, Rudolph made it clear that there were a few things his royal palate just couldn't be defaced with, such as, cabbage, porridge and potatoes - everything, in effect, that constituted the backbone of the Gymnasium's menu.

'The reason the authorities let him have his way so much though,' Samba told Sonia, 'is because he is so intelligent. He's first in all his courses. The white students can't understand it. He rarely finds the time to study, busy as he is telling unbelievable stories about his life among the beasts of the African jungle, and making constant forays into the city. His classmates just can't figure him out. They half believe him when he tells them that his success in the classroom is due to his mascot, a hideous skull that adorns his pillow whenever he's not in bed. Whenever there is an exam, Rudolph kneels down before it and pretends to pray to it for inspiration.'

Sonia held her sides with laughter and begged Samba to stop his narrating, 'Oh, I can't take any more' she cried wiping away tears of mirth. 'He's simply awful, that prince of yours, simply awful!'

For all his posing in school, Rudolph was a perfect gentleman once the gates of the Gymnasium were behind him. He carried out several love affairs around the country, his unlimited funds permitting him to travel extensively during the holidays. But his most torrid affair was with the dewy-eyed daughter of a *nouveau riche* merchant in Ulm itself. After knowing Rudolph for one year, this girl became determined to marry him and go with him to Africa at the end of his studies. The situation would have become a rather sticky one had the prince not had the bright idea of reminding his sweetheart that as the wife of a future African monarch, she would be only one among a hundred or so other Kamerunian-born queens, who would have equal claims as she on his favours. Try as the young lady would, she could not get Rudolph to promise that once in power he would change the marriage regulations in his country. She was up against that invincible monster - Tradition.

'The king is all-powerful, my darling' Rudolph told her.

'But there is one greater than he, and that is Tradition. To give up Tradition I must give up the throne.'

'Then give up the throne!' cried the maiden. 'What is an earthly crown compared to Our Love for each other?'

Rudolph was shocked, 'Give up the throne? To whom? I'm my father's only living son. The others all died in infancy.'

'Let some other family rule the country. Surely Our Love is worth the sacrifice!'

'None but the Manga Bells can rule Kamerun.' Rudolph replied in sepulchral tones.

The merchant's daughter wept, 'You don't love me!'

She threatened suicide, she threatened to drown herself in the blue Danube. 'I'll lock myself away in a nunnery!' she concluded.

Rudolph wiped away an invisible tear in his eye and held his darling close to his heart. 'If you do anything foolish I shall kill myself.' He kissed her rose pouting lips with fervour 'Wait, be patient, my darling. Between now and the time I have to leave Germany, we shall come up with a solution to our problem. You're too precious to me. I cannot imagine life without you.'

And so the love affair continued until the day the young prince left Germany without informing his secret fiancée of his departure.

Samba who, from the beginning, had been following a completely different course of studies from Rudolph and Felix in preparation for his military career, left in the Gymnasium a year before his friends to j enter a military academy in Cologne. For three years he and Sonia did not see each other until he emerged from the academy as a lieutenant in 1893 at the age of twenty-three.

Chapter Two

Throughout his life chief Nguni had been a warrior before anything else, his one ambition being the expansion of the kingdom his father, Maseko, had left him.

The vast harem he also inherited along with the Zulu throne preoccupied him not at all.

If he happened to think of his father's wives, it was in terms of women such as his mother and her mates, who had nurtured him and his brothers on their rocky way to boyhood and then watched them grow into men. How could he ever come to think of such women as these in sexual terms? True, there were young girls in his women's quarters -girls hardly out of their adolescence, children whom his father had deflowered and promptly lost interest in (as he grew more and more decrepit, Chief Maseko's hunger for young flesh grew into a frenzy).

Nguni left the bevy of females to their own devices, ignoring the young and pretty among them as well as old and venerated. He took his pleasure in warring. The daughters of conquered chiefs were his prey. During campaigns, there was always one who held his interest, one whom he kept in his tent each night he was not fighting. And when it was time to return to his palace, she was added to his harem, to spend the next several months invariably preparing to become a mother.

Two things happened to Nguni which, if they did not change his main ideal in life, at least gave it added dimension. The first of these was the arrival of the missionary explorer, Nigel Kohr, in Zululand in 1889. Attracted by stories of

Nguni's prowess and exploits, this adventurous German missionary left his Protestant settlement near Fort Frederick. With the help of two Zulu guides, he crossed the Drakenshergs and the Limpopo, penetrating into Nguni's Empire West of Lake Nyassa. Nguni's own palace, right on the shores of the lake, put the intrepid pastor in mind of Eden, or was it a fairyland from a story by the Grimm brothers? His brave heart burned with the seal of his divine mission as he imagined himself spreading the Good News among the primitive people of this enchanting land.

Between him and the Zulu chief there grew a friendship that culminated in Nigel Kohr's decision to make his home among the Zulus. Nguni, the Warlord, also became Nguni the scholar. Although the Zulu king never learnt to read and write, he spent many a long evening between campaigns with his white friend, imbibing the strange stories of white thought and way of life that Kohr recounted to him in fluent Zulu.

Nguni, at this time, was thirty-two years old, in his prime. The strength in his arm was equated to that of an iroko tree. His rule extended over a vast kingdom of conquered tribes who had been forced into allegiance to him.

In 1894, the second significant event of Nguni's life occurred. He was besieged by a group of Katangan warriors who were fleeing South-eastwards from the Congo forest into his domain, driven by white invaders who had expelled them from their own land.

By the end of that year, the Katangans had been subjected by the Zulus except for one regiment - the strongest, led by a troop of women fighters - Amazons who withdrew into a natural hill fortress at Thaba Bosiu in the mountains each time Nguni's army attacked them. Whenever the Zulus decided to leave the women to their own devices on their mountain hideout, they descended on the neighbouring peoples raiding and plundering until an army had to be sent out against them. At which point the females would flee to their mountain citadel, leaving the frustrated Zulu king at his wits end as to what to do to remove this thorn in his royal flesh.

It was the Rev. Kohr who found a solution to the problem after two long years of incessant fighting and stalemate between Nguni and the Katangan warriors.

'What is most likely to soften the heart of the toughest female on this earth?' asked the preacher.

'A child,' replied chief Nguni without the slightest hesitation.

'We shall use a child to entrap these lionnesses.' said the Pastor.

Nguni was all ears. Together, he and Kohr chose one out of the hundreds of palace children - a bright girl of scarcely nine years of age, and travelled with her to the village of Sotho, ravaged by the constant raids of the Katangans. In the dead of a black night, Nguni and the little girl camped as close to Thaba Bosiu as they dared without alerting the occupants of the fortress.

Just before cockcrow next morning, the women on the mountain the pitiful wailing of a child coming up from some way up the hillside. Could it be a child that had lost its way among the hills and woods? If so it would just have to wander back down to its people. But the crying seemed to rise from one particular spot. The sound was unmistakably that of a child in agony calling out to its mother. For an hour the plucky little Zulu girl kept up her cry for help while Nguni crouched hidden in a bush a few feet away from her, waiting. Had Rev. Kohr surmised correctly or were these tigresses too hardened in their warring hearts to be moved by such a common place emotion as pity? A bright sun now stood at a thirty-degree angle in the sky overhead. It glistened on the wet green foliage each drop of dew reflecting the world in bewitching colour.

Nguni had heard no sound. His watchful eye was steadily trained on the child before him. Suddenly, he became aware of a footfall - two slender sandaled feet, cowries at their ankles rested on the ground before the weeping youngster.

'Aie - Aie - Aie - my fo-o-t!' called the child.

The woman, as she descended the hill, had been keeping a darting eye on the surrounding grounds. But a few steps away from the prone figure, her vigilance momentarily flagged as her eyes alighted on the horrible scene at her feet. The apparently suffering child had been caught in a lion's trap, her bleeding left leg held between the sharp teeth of the vicious snare, the earth around the trap seemed to have soaked the blood until it could soak no more. A puddle of old blood reflected the sun in a dingy glow - a sight to wrench the stoniest of hearts.

Nguni gave the woman no time. Tensed like a bow, he sprang in a frog's leap high above his sheltering brambles, short fighting spear in hand, and collided onto the Amazon's back even as she made to crouch down beside the entrapped girl. Arrows flex above their heads as Ngum drew the woman down onto the grass with himself underneath her. His left hand held her at the nape of her neck in a death grip while both knees held her arms imprisoned at her sides. His adversary made no sound as the chief raised both him and herself to kneeling positions, she in front of him, both facing the bushes above them. Brandishing his short spear and pointing it at the Amazon's throat, he called out to his enemies above not to shoot at the risk of having him kill his captive.

'Give yourselves up,' shouted Nguni, 'or she dies!'

Far down below him he could hear his soldiers approaching warily up the hillside.

'Not a shot,' cried Ngum to the invisible women above him, 'or else!'

And still the prisoner in his grip made no sound, showed no resistance. But Nguni did not relax. Slowly he pulled her up with him to a standing position. Abruptly, she crouched half-way down and heaved with her rear. But Nguni was a split second quicker than her. The shove, which had been meant to send him flying above her head to the ground at her feet so that she could get above him, misfired. The two of them fell on their backs, she still on top, still imprisoned in his arms. Nguni helped her and himself to their feet once more.

His knees still held her prisoner. His left arm encircled her chest from shoulder to shoulder. As yet she had made no sound, but he could feel the pressure of her firm breasts rising and falling beneath his unrelenting arm, the round buttocks pressing against his groin. He began to enjoy the whole setup. He had never given shape of form to the band of women who had pestered him for so many months. But even if had done so, he surely would not have endowed them with normal womanly attributes such as curves and shapes capable of sending the blood pulsating hotly through a man's veins.

His men were coming closer. The leaves parted in the bushes above him and a girl appeared. She looked barely fourteen years old and was dressed in baggy animal-skin shorts and a short sleeve - less top that left her midriff bare. She threw down her bow, her bag of arrows, her pouch of knives, darts, and spear. Then she flung her arms wide apart to show that she was no longer armed. Immediately, Nguni's captive barked out what seemed to be an order for her to go back into hiding. The girl shook her head defiantly, tears rolling down her cheeks. The prisoners started to speak again but before she had uttered two words, more women came out of the surrounding, trees, throwing down their weapons while the hostage, whom Nguni now began to suspect was their leader, let flow a spate of angry words in their Bantu dialect which was not completely foreign to Nguni. He was able to gather that the leader was berating her band for giving themselves up so easily. She would preferred to die if the other Amazons could have saved them-selves.

Nguni's soldiers now proceeded to tie up the prisoners in readiness for the descent into Sotho.

In the bridal chamber, Zara cocked an ear at the music assailing her from all around the palace. A sumptuously appointed room, heady with the smell of lavender and incense.

A bed fit for a king. And it was the king's bed. Her lips curled. She "was waiting for him. The beads, the flimsy white cotton robe, the jars of scent and oils, all the accoutrements brought here by the old palace wives to shower on her in preparation for their Lord and Master - they all lay strewn on the floor where they had fallen as, with one furious sweep of the hand, Zara had sent them flying, daring any of the women to touch her. They had all dispersed, no match for the demon she had become in her fury?

The beaded door curtain parted to make passage for Nguni, who came in dressed only in a white flowing loincloth, and looking mellow from the day's feasting and merry making. A fine figure of a man, he stood tall, dark, muscled - the epitome of Zulu malehood. Nguni's deep-set eyes took in the spectacle of the incensed female faced him across the room, unflinching eyes glaring at him. She was young. The Zulu chief judged her to be no older than sixteen. She stood feet apart, arms akimbo, waiting, her stance spelling defiance. Imitating her, he also placed a hand on either hip before approaching her.

For a charged moment they stared into each other's eyes. Then, in one swift movement, Nguni had her arms pinioned behind her in a cruel grip.

'You're no match for me, beautiful tigress,' he smiled at her.

She spat into his face. Nguni tendered two ringing slaps
to each side of her face before wiping his.

'You're no man, Mighty Nguni.' she hissed at him. 'If I
am your captive today, it is not by fair and honourable
combat. For two years I defied you. I plundered your land
and laid it to waste. The only way you could reach me was
by resorting to unmanly trickery and cowardly device. In a
thousand years the griots will still be singing your name as
the Zulu chief who could not face a troop of women in
honest battle.'

The self-satisfied smile had been wiped away from Nguni's
face. The deep-set eyes were still On her but their look was
as impenetrable as a muddy pool. She knew she had hurt
him in a tender spot - his male pride - and she was exultant.

'Your tongue is quick to spit out venom little viper.' He
was twisting her arms almost out of their sockets bringing
tears of pain to her defiant eyes.

'Would you care to face me in single combat?' demanded
the Zulu chief.

'Yes!' she cried passionately. 'Oh, yes! Name your time
and place. I am ready to meet you on equal terms, to fight
in deadliest combat.'

He flung her away from him. 'You give yourself too
much consequ-ence, young girl. I should not stop to give a
woman that much honour.'

'Ah, but I was of enough consequence to incite you to
subterfuge and unmanly cunning,' she retorted.

'Even as I would set a trap to snare a pestering house rat.'

'No matter. My followers and I have yet to see the bravery
of your army, Chief Nguni. Whatever you get from me shall
have to be ravished from me. Maybe then only might I see
some of that famed Nguni prowess in action.'

Nguni took a good look at her. Tall, dark-skinned brown-
eyed, her hair short-cropped, she wore no ornament except
for the cowry beads around her ankles. Although she had

washed and cleaned herself, she was still dressed in the baggy shorts and top that seemed to have been their uniform.

No man, much less a woman, had ever dared speak so boldly to Chief Nguni, and it was certain none other would ever again defy him in this manner. But the novelty of the situation intrigued him.

Also, the more he saw of the girl the more he saw to whet his appetite. Any other woman would have been sent to the stake for saying much less than Zara had said to him today. Nguni decided that he would derive more pleasure in taming this wild pony than in killing it. He went out, leaving her alone in the room.

The conversation, the strangest he had ever held with a female, kept ringing in his head. Excepting his mother, he could not remember ever having spoken this long with any woman. What was the world coming to? This girl actually dared look him in the eye and challenge him to a combat! As the Zulu chief told his missionary friend next day, these Amazons must hail from a barbaric tribe. But he welcomed the challenge.

'It shall be my pleasure,' announced the king, 'to teach her that warrior or no warrior, she is still but a woman.'

The Reverend made no reply, but the glint in his eyes was unmistak-able.

'What are you laughing at?' bristled the Zulu warlord.

'I was just thinking what a fine specimen of health and beauty Zara is,' replied the Pastor innocently.

'Indeed, you are correct,' agreed the chief. 'Such proud breasts! A body like a sculpture in mahogany. Surely a woman fit to bear the king's heirs!'

Reverend Kohr coughed delicately, 'Surely a woman well worth humouring.'

'For the greater pleasure of subduing:' concluded the chief.

A cool evening breeze, blowing across like Nyassa. Eucalyptus and fir murmuring in the breeze. Zara, in spite of herself, is charmed by the king's domain. The grounds surrounding the palace is half wilderness, half garden. She spends hours roaming the woods, spying bashful rabbits, graceful antelopes, zebras, wild fowl that watch her but keep out of her way.

Her hosts have assured her that no dangerous animal lives around the palace. As long as she did not step on a snake she was in no danger, and snake usually kept their distance.

This evening, she sits on the lakeside alone, her eyes scanning the wide expanse of water, lost in thought. Nguni, on horseback, is already twenty feet away before she realises she is no longer alone. She turns to look at him for a second before returning her gaze to the lake. The chief dismounts and tethers his horse to a tree trunk. As he approaches her, he wonders what thoughts go through that wilful head. Surely not the normal thoughts of an ordinary woman. What is it like in the land she comes from? He sits beside her, his mind jostling with questions.

What kind of relationship exists between man and woman when the female is also trained to fight like a man? This troop of Amazons has completely upset Nguni's notions on womankind. Zara was a fine soldier; she possessed brute strength, could wrestle as well as the next Zulu warrior. On the other hand, Nguni had only to close his eyes to conjure up this same Zara in a completely different setting. He could imagine her all sweetness and gentleness, a son in her arms sucking at a full ripe breast. Zara fulfilled, happy to be the mother of some deserving man's sons. So what was the difference between these female fighters and other women? Just as Zara could have been a wife and mother, so, he supposed, could his mother and other Zulu women have been brought up to be soldiers.

After a few moments of silence between them, Nguni could not restrain his curiosity.

'Tell me, Zara, What is it like in the country you hail from?'

She turned her gaze on him with a knowing smile on her lips which told him she understood the questions jogging his brain.

'In Katanga, we Bantus are even greater warriors than the Zulus.'

Again this belittling of him and his people. But Nguni's curiosity had the better of him. He let it go as Zara continued speaking.

'The first daughter of every Queen is handed over to the army. Not only does she become a soldier, she is consecrated to Mpala, the God of war. The whole nation knows that for male hands to defile a Kazi, Mpala's anointed, by touching her, is to bring down the god's anger on the people for seven consecutive years, during which they shall suffer unremitting defeat at the hands of their enemies. My sisters and I were taken from our mothers at the age of seven. We form an elite regiment in our father's army.' She realised she was speaking in the present tense. 'We formed an elite regiment in the king's army.'

So! she was a princess as well as soldier!

'We lived the rest of our lives in barracks far from the palace and from the villagers.'

Nguni's mind boggled. What would a group of nubile young women think of and dream of, cut off from normal life, deprived of male company, steeped only in the study of war? Still, he liked the idea of her being as yet untouched.

'Were you happy?' he wanted to know.

'It is our way of life.'

'Still, no-one can be a soldier all his life - not even a man. Surely your tradition allowed for the fact that, as women, the Kazis had other contributions to make to the society.'

48

She turned a mocking smile on him. 'Believe me, the absence of our contributions would hardly have occasioned any great loss for the country. We were only our mothers' first daughters. If you think that of the over six hundred women who make up the king's harem, each is likely to have at least seven children and most of them girls, you will agree that our services could well be dispensed with as far as procreation was concerned. However, to answer your question, we are all released from military service at the age of twenty-five. All, that is, except for the Kabuzi, or leader of the regiment. The Kabuzi's life is the regiment. It Js she who leads in battle; she it is who stays on to admit and train new Kazis when they reach the age of recruitment. Once every twenty years, or if a Kabuzi dies prematurely, a new one is chosen to replace her.'

'And her sisters who leave?'

'Oh, they enter traditional lives. The king usually marries them off to his various provincial governors and army officers.'

'Where I imagine they have no small hand in directing the defence of their country's borders.' Nguni concluded drily.

'If their Lords and Masters see nothing wrong in taking advantage of their experience and know-how.' Zara's tone was equally dry. Then she added. 'I had been chosen to replace our old Kabuzi who was nearing , the age of retirement.'

Nguni looked sharply in her direction. But her face remained impassive, almost stern. The Zulu king could not reconcile himself to the notion. She sat there talking to him like a man, voice clear and firm while he, like a child listening to the village bard, hung on her every word. She fascinated him, this man-woman. What savages these Katangans were to stifle a woman's natural instincts. It was an outrage against nature. They were trying to create monsters, neither female nor male, unthinking things trained to do only one thing in life - fight.

49

Far on the opposite shores of the lake, the fishermen were returning home. The lakeshore was a busy market place at this time of day, women buying not only fish but spices and condiments for the family's evening meal. Zara appeared absorbed by the spectacle. Watching her detached profile in the glowing evening sun, Nguni wondered if she ever saw herself as an actor in one of these mundane scenes.

Zara, the Kabuzi-elect. He wanted to know more and more about the strange life she had led.

'And so you haven't seen your family since the age of seven?'

'Nothing so drastic. We took turns - each month a group of Kazis was allowed to go home for the new moon.'

'And the Kabuzi?'

'She never leaves the barracks except to go to war. Mpala is a jealous god.'

'Do you regret being deprived of the opportunity of living a Kabuzi's life?'

'I would have been happy. It is a great honour to be chosen/

'Your companions are getting used to the different kind of life they have found here.'

Zara made no answer, merely staring straight ahead of her.

'In fact they are happy.' Nguni insisted. 'They enjoy the company of the young men. They are learning to be women.'

'I am happy for them.'

He wanted to ask her why she wasn't softening up like her sisters had done. Why always this unbending attitude of mind? Nguni was not sure what she might do. He might wake up one morning to find that she had taken off on her own, flown, lost forever to him. And yet, he would put no guard on her. She was free to roam as she chose. The gates of his palace stood wide open - she could walk in and out as she pleased. On Nigel Kohr's advice, he had not spoken to her again after the tense interview in the bridal chamber.

'She is a wild young thing.' said the priest. 'Do not hem her in, and, above all, do not importune her. In fact, it would do no harm to make her feel you have lost interest in her.'

Thus the two men plotted and planned her conquest as if she were a citadel under their siege. By now Nguni was determined the only way he would have her was if she gave herself to him of her own free will.

'Would you like to listen to a story?' he asked her. 'Nigel told it to me.

A smile of disdain played on her lips. 'The Reverend tells fascinating stories. But beware of him.'

'Why? How can he harm me? He is all alone here amongst us, Zulus. He can do nothing without my consent. Do you find his preachings dangerous? On the contrary, I find his constant talk about this God of his fascinating. Do you know what he says? He says black men and white men both come from this one God of his. We all come from one source. Isn't that fascinating? Personally, I find it a bit hard to swallow.'

She turned a pitying look on him, 'Poor my lord, silence that evil white tongue at once before greater harm befalls you. His words of love have no meaning. None at all. Kill him and never again as long as you live welcome another white man into your domain!'

The urgency in her voice startled him.

'Listen,' she said. 'I shall tell you a story, a story about the white man. Once in Africa, there lived a powerful king, ruler of a brave people who lived in peace with their neighbours. Until one day there arrived a group of white traders, tattered and battered. They were escaping from the army of another African chief who had attacked and killed some of the members of the white band of traders. So they said. They sought refuge and hospitality from this chief until such a time as they could organise themselves again to continue their journey to the seacoast where their brothers awaited them. Hospitality was given them. Their wounds were tended to, and when they "were ready to leave, this great king showered them with gifts - ivory and precious stones, with a team of twenty carriers to see the white men to their destination.' Here Zara's voice broke, but she sat up straighter gazing with greater intensity across the lake.

'Two moons passed, then three. The mothers of those young carriers waited in vain for their sons to return. In the fourth month of their absence, the leader of the white traders reappeared at the village alone. Where were the young men? Not to worry, the white man told the villagers, the youths had stayed at the coast longer than had been planned. The white men had been so grateful to them that they had insisted that the twenty youths spend a couple of months with them as guests of honour at their trading post. They were about a week's journey away from their home now, travelling slowly because they were once more laden with gifts from their white friends to the chief. The chief asked no more questions. Wasn't this white man now his brother? Hadn't he eaten from the same place and drunk from the same cup as he? Had he not nursed the white man's battle wounds, hidden mm from his pursuers? There was a banquet held that night and the king went to sleep with a smile on his face.

'He was woken up very early the next morning before cockcrow by sounds of shouting and thunder. When he stepped out of his hut, it was to collide into a troop of strange-looking soldiers coming to fetch him. What was this? He looked for his white friend and spied him at the palace gates, directing more and more foreign soldiers to strategic points or the village. His own soldiers were already gathered in a group, bound hand and foot in heavy chains. His white friend passed him by without a glance. Young men and women were being added to the line of chained men. Those who showed the least sign of resistance were instantly killed by a fire - breathing weapon that each white soldier carried.'

Zara paused for breath, when she took up the thread of her story again, her voice was calmer, even subdued.

'A group of Kazis who reached the village on the usual monthly leave brought us the news of the ravage. Those not carried away by the white traders had been killed. Only a few old men and women, a handful of babies were left to tell the story of the plunder. Our father had, of course, been killed.' She stopped.

Her listener was dumbfounded. 'But how did you come to reach Zulu land?'

'After burying our dead, we waited for the white people. We now understood them. We knew they would return. They had taken our men and women. They would come back for the ivory and gold, the copper and diamonds. Far away in our barracks, we watched the village and waited till they came. And did they ever come. My Mother!' Zara was scarcely aware of Nguni's presence as her memory carried her into the past.

Caravan load upon caravan load of white, brown and black men. It was plain to the spying Kazis that these people were coming to stay. In a week, buildings were erected. The men started digging and digging, the blacks working while the whites strode up and down barking out orders, brandishing evil-looking whips, and soldiers patrolled, rifles slung over their shoulders. Sad to say, none of the gang of working blacks was a member of Zara's old village. The Kazis watched and laid out their plan of action. They came to understand the mechanism of the white man's guns. They learnt where their extra arms were stored.

'There were a hundred and twenty of us in those barracks. Out of this number, sixty were full - fledged soldiers with battle experience. The day we descended on those strangers, it was like the eruption of a volcano. Our only regret was that there were so few white people there for us to butcher. But there were also the Arabs, the yellow ones, with whom the white traders worked hand in hand and who helped the white men humiliate our kind.

'Two hours after the middle of the night, thirty of us surrounded the small cabin where their arms were kept. Each of us took possession of a gun. We had learnt, from watching them undetected for four months, how to load them. As for operating them, that was child's play. The white men all slept together at a distance from their slaves, so it was easy to mount a surprise attack on them. They didn't stand a chance. The few who made for the arsenal were met with shots from the thirty Kazis surrounding the cabin.'

By now there was a bright moon shining above the two figures by the lakeside. Its reflection on the still lake lighted up the surrounding woods yet created a special sort of intimacy between Zara and the Zulu which neither was in any hurry to disturb. Each could see the other as clearly as if the dark had not yet descended. For the first time in his life Nguni was looking at a woman with awe in his eyes. He felt positively humbled in the presence of this amazing girl who could sit by his side and calmly describe a battle as if it was just part of the day's job.

She went on with her story, 'Our Kabuzi routed all the slaves who had been working for the white men and we took them with us to our barracks. We also took all the white man's arms, the plan was that we would train the men to fight and then join together with them to construct a new village - have children and build another society to replace that which was now lost forever.

But we were not clever enough. It never occurred to us that the white men's friends would come looking for them, discover their dead bodies and set out in search of us. That is what happened. They surprised us even as we had surprised their brothers.

We used their guns against them, but this time they came with bigger heavier weapons which rolled before them on wheels sprouting out bigger fires - our guns were no match for them. They could stand at a distance and throw objects in our direction which would set the ground underneath our feet trembling as in an earthquake, the trees and grass around us bursting into sudden flame. We were all killed except for the few Kazis I managed to lead across the black forest into your land.'

When Nguni next looked into Zara's face, two large tears were rolling down her smooth cheeks. There was a lump in his throat as large as his fist. He managed to swallow it down somewhat into his queasy stomach and reach out a forthcoming hand to the lonely girl at his side. His gesture was purely paternal and she did not before repulse him.

'There, there child, you have no more reason to fear or mistrust. We offer you friendship and a home. Stay among us and become of us or, if that does not please you, choose any land you want in my Empire and live your own lives apart from us if that is your wish.'

Before Zara could make a reply a horseman came galloping up behind them. Dismounting hastily, he threw himself on all fours before the King in the traditional greeting reserved for monarchs, apologising abjectly for intruding upon the king's privacy. Zara and the chief had sprung to their feet at the horseman's approach and now stood looking down at him.

'Rise Shulele,' ordered the king recognising his chief bodyguard. 'I trust the palace is not under siege.'

'Not that serious yet, my Lord.' replied the soldier coming to attention. 'But an emissary from Xhosaland has just arrived with an urgent plea from the governor, Ngqrika, for reinforcements. The white settlers on Cape Colony have forced the Xhosa chief, Ndlambe, out of the Western side of the Great Fish river. They now want to establish the river as the boundary between their colony and your conquered Xhosa territory.

Ndlambe is powerless against this British onslaught and Ngqrika's forces are already depleted from earlier clashes with the Boers in this same area. They need urgent help to repulse the white advancement.'

Nguni let fall an oath. 'Very well, Shulele. Return to the palace and tell Kilamiuzu, my lieutenant, to get the troops ready to leave tomor-row before dawn. We shall pick up more troops as we go along. I am leading this expedition myself. Now go!'

Shulele kissed the ground at his master's feet and leapt away on his horse.

Nguni turned to the girl at his side, 'Shall I find you here when I return?'

'My Lord' replied Zara. 'Let me go with you. I can be of no mean assistance to you, and it would give me such great pleasure to face the white man again.'

But Nguni would not hear of it. 'Stay home, Zara, and learn to do something other than fighting.' What was this obsession she had with warring? Could she find interest in nothing else?

He was determined not to let her see a battlefield again if he could help it.

'Listen,' he coaxed. 'I will leave my palace and the village in the care of you and your sisters. Defend it while I am away.'

'My sisters can do that with or without me. Take me with you.'

'No!'

'Let me assuage some of my pain by doing battle against my enemies. Let me come with you!'

Nguni had leapt into his saddle 'Look,' he smiled down into the girl's upturned face. 'I promise to bring back no less than twenty white prisoners for you to torture to your heart's content before killing them.' And he was off at a gallop.

'It is not the same thing!' Zara called after him.

He did not hear her.

'It is not the same thing,' she repeated to herself, and set off after the chief. Ndlambe and Nguni sat huddled around a small camp-fire in front of the king's tent. Around them similar fires burned in the cool night, warming the thousands of warriors the Zulu chief had brought with him to the Xhosa front two days before. The sturdy figure of Ngqrika materialised out of the shadows as he marched with swift steps to join the two men by the fire. He was a stocky-built twenty-five year-old warrior of medium height, with an open intelligent-looking face. Nguni motioned him to a low stool by his side, the governor rubbed his palms together holding his hands out towards the flames.

'There's some good news, my Lord. One of my spies, a slave in the household of a Boer family, reports that the British have taken over the entire settlement of Cape Colony. The Boers no longer have the protection of their Dutch Government, and the British are more sympathetic towards the plight of our people. The reason behind the sudden halt in British advancement into our territory is that the Boers have rebelled against British rule, and are trying to establish an independent state of their own. For the past week, the Boers have been engaged in defending themselves against British soldiers sent to quell the revolt.'

'Beautiful!' exclaimed the Zulu chief. 'This is our chance. We shall hasten to strike the Boers from behind and push them back from the other side of the Fish river. The river as well as the land surrounding it belongs to us.' He turned to Ndlambe. 'I know the Fish river and the adjoining land play an important role in your lives.'

'It is the best pastureland in the country, my Lord, and we, Xhosas, are mainly cattle rearers.'

Nguni nodded in understanding.

'Those fatherless sons of witches!' Ndlambe flared. 'Where did they spring from? How dare they quarrel over land that belongs to neither of them? Oh, if our fathers could see the harm they did in ever letting the white man set foot on African soil!'

Shut up, Ndlambe!' ordered his overlord. 'Wailing will get you nowhere.'

Are we animals then to be routed, and fenced in, and allowed no freedom of movement?' Ndlambe's nomadic soul was slowly being asphyxiated by the restrictions the white invasion had imposed on the movements of his tribe. The Zulus had conquered him but still left him in his land as long as he pledged allegiance to them. With the new European pressure, he could move neither eastwards where he would collide with other tribes, nor southwards where the treacherous ocean lay. The only direction left open to him was the hills, and who ever heard of cows scaling hills?

Ngqrika's voice addressing Nguni cut through Ndlambe's dark thoughts. 'My Lord, these Boers are an evil people. To them the black men are no better than cattle, than beasts of burden.'

'I know, I know,' replied Nguni.

How many times had the Zulu chief gone over and over the Boer mind with his friend Nigel. The German had taken pains to explain the difference between Boers and other while men, completely dissociating himself not only from Boers but from the general colonialist minded white hoard intent on plundering the African continent.

The missionary had kept his cool, refusing the let Nguni's tauntings and abuses of the white race ruffle him. He was in Africa for a different purpose and was concerned only with letting the Zulu chief understand that he and others like him were bringing something to Africa and asking nothing in return.

At the end of Nigel Kohr's lengthy explanations on Boer Philosophy, Nguni had come to the conclusion that they were just a bunch of lazy people whose primary purpose in life was finding other people to do their work for them. But being of a religious bent, they had to justify their laziness by branding the black man an inferior species to whom the usual rules governing relationships between human beings did not apply.

His thoughts swung to Zara and her insatiable thirst for white blood. You heard stories of the white man's greed, tales of his inhumanity towards blacks and somehow it all seemed so remote. These things happened, yes, but to others only, not to you. Even while he argued and locked verbal horns with Nigel Kohr over the black/white conflict, Nguni never really envisaged the possibility of one day confronting this racial plague himself. When he had conquered Xhosaland, the tiny colony of Boers living in Graaf Reinct had been the least of his worries. He had assumed that both the Boers and the Xhosas would be careful to keep out of each other's way. It now appeared, however, that the indolent Boers would never leave the Africans alone. They seized Xhosa cattle with impunity and then captured the Xhosas themselves for use as slaves.

And now the British had also joined in the fray. In his heart Nguni knew that he could never win the war against the white colonists. His spears and arrows were no match for European weapons. But that was no reason not to put up a fight. He would win the few battles he could before backing out. And so that night he set his men loose on the Boers.

It was a night of carnage. Nguni had instructed his men to spare nobody - man, woman or child. The Boers, exhausted and demoralised from their unfruitful encounter with the British Government, were found in their beds by the angry Zulus and methodically butchered. The few British soldiers who were patrolling the Dutch settlement were taken entirely unawares. Graaff Reinet was burned to the ground before news reached the British Cape Government. Nguni's troops moved to the eastern shore of the Fish river to await the inevitable reprisals.

Two days later, early in the morning, Ngqrika brought news to Nguni that an unknown Zulu rider had informed him of the approach of English forces.

'They spent the night at Uitenhage, my Lord, and are now headed for Great Fish. My informant believes they will attack us this very night from the south.'

'Who brought this information?'

'He would not even descend from his horse my Lord, merely warning us to expect heavy artillery.'

That night, when the British troops arrived, they found part of the Zulu army on the river banks. While the white army was engaged in battle with these, the rest of Nguni's warriors emerged from the forests behind the foreign army raining poisoned arrows on them.

Nguni knew he stood no chance of winning. His aim, therefore, was to cause as much damage to the colonist army as he could before retreating. As his opponents turned to train their awful weapons on his warriors, he barked out the order for his men to retreat. He was himself crawling backwards into the bushes. It was as he stood up to run the final paces into the woods that a bullet caught him between the shoulder blades. He fell with a cry of agony. Immediately two strong arms half carried, half dragged him farther away into the forest. The pain sent stars flying across his brain, he tried to cry out once more, but his lips felt like lead. He heard a familiar voice call out for help in lifting him. Then the darkness engulfed him.

He woke up to the sound of a flute playing, sunlight streaming through the wide-open entrance of his tent. He was lying on his stomach on a soft pile of animal skins and dried grass. His whole back throbbed with pain and he did not even attempt to -change his position.

A shadow fell across the entrance, and Zara came in carrying a small bouquet of leaves. Their eyes met.

'You're awake, my Lord!'

'Zara!' Where in the world was he?

She placed her bundle carefully on the floor then knelt beside him to reel his forehead with her palm. 'Thank Heavens, the fever has fallen! How do you feel?'

'Fine,' he lied. 'But, what are you doing here? Or am I still dreaming?'

'We're halfway between your palace and Xhosaland. You have been very ill and so we have been obliged to camp in this forest until you're better.'

Then memory came back to his dulled brain. 'You were at Great Fish!'

'Yes, my Lord. I picked you up when you fell. Ngqrika is with us. Let me call for him.'

She stood at the tent door and hollered for the young governor, the fluting stopped. In a minute, Ngqrika was beside her. Together they removed the dressing from Nguni's wound. It was responding well to the freshly-mixed medicine the chief's friend applied on it every day. Ngqrika untied a corner of his loincloth and showed Nguni the bullet he had extracted from the wound.

'Fortunately, it lodged in a muscle. No bone was touched. But you were delirious from fever as well as me wound, so we thought it best to camp here until you were strong enough to move again. Most of the warriors have gone on before us, my Lord. We have only some thirty men guarding our caravan.'

'Ndlambe and the Xhosas?'

'Zara and myself took the liberty of instructing Ndlambe to move his people away from the Fish river. The white men want it and there is nothing we can do. The added population is going to put a lot of pressure on the Tembus who are already over-populated, but your Majesty will find a solution to the problem as soon as you are yourself again.'

'Zara?'

Ngqrika grinned, 'Were it not for her, my Lord, there's no saying what might have happened. She it was who saw you fall and dragged you into the bushes before calling for help.'

Zara, who had been pounding her bundle of leaves in a little hand mortar now interrupted. 'You're tired, my Lord. There will be time enough to answer your questions when you're stronger.' She turned to Ngqrika. 'No more talk. The dressing for his wound is ready. Let's wash him, feed him and let him rest.' Nguni was too weak to protest.

Two weeks later, feeling much better, the Zulu chief was out wild fowl hunting with Zara. Armed with a sling, the girl led the way, her trained eyes searching the bushes for the familiar grey-speckled birds. Nguni followed close behind carrying a pouch of pebbles - ammunition for Zara's sling. But, instead of keeping his eyes on the bushes as Zara was doing, the Zulu chief was engrossed in admiring the girl's legs and bottom as she advanced stealthily ahead of him.

Spotting one of the birds standing at the base of a stunted palm tree, Zara stopped short, turning a finger to her lips to warn Nguni. The chief, however, had not been attentive. Before he knew Zara had stopped, he had collided into her, toppling both himself and her.

From their positions on the ground, they watched the alerted bird fly away with a raucous cackle. Zara was maddened. Nguni hastily pulled himself off her, apologising shamefacedly for his clumsiness.

'I'm sorry, really I am. Oh!' The pouch of pebbles had slipped from Nguni's hand, spilling its contents in the wild under bush.

It was too much for Zara. She burst into a peal of laughter, collapsing onto the grass as Nguni searched in vain for the small stones, in the thick undergrowth. It wasn't long before he had joined in her amuse-ment, laughing until his not-yet-healed wound started smarting. Zara was up like a shot at the sight of his slight grimace. She knelt behind him and laid a hand on his shoulder.

'Oh, you poor one, you've hurt yourself! Is it bad?'

Receiving no answer, she bent forward bringing her face to within an
inch of his, 'My Lord!'

Nguni's eyes bore into hers holding her captive. Taking the hand she had placed on his shoulder he pulled her down to sit on his lap. She waited for him to speak.

'Zara!'

He held out a hand and she placed hers in it. His other hand slid up and down her forearm.

'Since I've seen you, Zara, I want no other woman.'

She looked intently into his face without speaking.

'If someone stole you away from me, Zara, I would take my whole army and search for you till I found you - that's how important you are to me.'

She smiled, her eyes unwavering, 'And if someone took me away from you, my Lord, I would die rather than give myself to him.'

Nguni sank his head onto her bosom, 'You shall be my Queen, my only woman till the day I die.'

Then they were lying on the grass her vibrant body trembling as he touched her.

The next week they were back in the woods tracking birds once again. This time, Nguni held his own sling as they stalked a huge peacock they had sighted half an hour before. It was a magnificent bird, very much aware of its beauty as it strutted, spreading first one glossy wing, then the other, so that it caught the sun in a million colours.

'Oh, it is so-o beautiful!' breathed Zara. 'It would be a crime to hurt it. Let's try to catch it. We'll take it home with us and let it loose in the palace woods.'

'And name it Zara after my beautiful, proud, Queen.'

'And you'll have no other queen but her?'

'I swear it by my dear dead father's soul!' He placed a hand on the dearly-loved head. 'Your sons only shall be my heirs. No others shall have the right to call me father.'

'And when you ride out to war, then shall your queen languish, alone at home?'

'Never!'

Her triumphant laughter filled the woods. 'You see now, my Lord, that being a warrior has not prevented me from being a woman!'

Nguni's tone was solemn as he said, 'You are the bravest warrior in my army.'

There came a rushing sound above their heads and they looked up to see the peacock disappearing farther from them into the jungle.

They retraced their steps to the camp after plucking a basketful of berries and guava for their companions. Nguni's wound was now at a stage where he felt they could start off for home any day soon.

He burned to show Nigel the progress he had made with Zara, and to tell the European about the special feelings he had for her. Above all, he longed to publicly proclaim her his Queen. Oh, they would have a unique relationship, for here was a woman with whom he could talk, with whom he could go hunting or fighting, the perfect companion. They would live like two brothers and yet be lovers.

The wonder of it all took his breath away and he felt like kneeling to kiss her feet in gratefulness for the light she had brought into his life. There was no other woman like her in the world. The gods had made this one specially for him and sent her to him in this strange manner in recompense for some good deed his father or one of his ancestors had done in his life. He must discuss it with Nigel. For his part, he could not see what he could have done to deserve such a blessing.

Zara was running ahead of him as they neared the camp, her basket of fruit at her hip, a happy child, so different from the bitter rebellious girl he had captured that distant day on the slopes of Thaba Bosiu. 'Ngqika, Ngqrika!' she called as they reached camp. She stopped short suddenly, her body stiffening. Nguni ran up to her as Ngqika's voice reached them, urgent, strange.

'Run, Zara, run!'

Nguni's blood froze as he also surveyed the scene before them. A team of horsemen surrounded the camp, guns in hand, herding his small team of warriors together like sheep. One or two bodies lay in the dust unmoving, unmistakably dead. Who were the horsemen? They had seen the newcomers and now four of them came galloping hotly in their direction, white robes flapping in the wind, guns at the ready.

Nguni took the girl's hand and held it firmly as she started backing away from the riders.

'It's no use, Zara. We cannot escape them.'

She saw his reasoning and stood up straight beside him, waiting for the men to reach them. When they came up, Nguni saw they were Arabs - tall, slight of build and fair-skinned. They drew up their horses and examined the man and the girl.

'A woman, eh?' said one of the riders in broken Zulu. 'How many more of you are hiding in the forest?' They made no reply. 'Of course they won't say,' said another.

'Let's take these two to the camp. We'll search the forest later. Go on, move! Let's join your friends.'

They shoved the captives ahead with the butts of their guns. Zara was trembling as she stumbled towards the camp.

Two of Nguni's warriors lay dead on the ground and Ngqrika, not yet dead, lay bleeding beneath a tree. Seeing him, Nguni dropped Zara's hand and ran to kneel beside his young friend. He had been shot in the breast and the life was seeping out of him.

The young man looked into his chief's eyes. 'Do not pity me, my Lord. This is my escape. These men are Arab traders looking for slaves to sell to the white man. Alas, what shall become of the Zulus? You shall never see your people again.'

A long whip, wielded by one of the horsemen, cracked across Nguni's back as he continued to kneel above his dying countryman. Zara screamed as she saw the blood oozing out of the chief's re-opened wound. As she ran up to him, rough hands jerked her back.

The rest of the Zulu prisoners were already being shackled at the ankle to a heavy clanging iron chain their hands tied behind them. They all stood with heads bowed as if afraid to look on the humiliation of their king.

Nguni, blind with rage sprang up with a demented cry and in one bound landed in the saddle behind his assailant, his fingers twining around the man's throat in a death grip. The rest of the Arabs gathered around them in confusion, pulling the Zulu chief by the leg in an effort to unseat him. But when Nguni toppled off the horse, the horseman came down with him still held in the Zulu's deadly embrace. The Arab's eyes were now popping out of his head, his tongue stealing slowly out in a macabre smile. As if in concert, the rest of his companions lifted their guns, pointing them at the chief's bleeding back.

'No-oo-o-oP Zara's voice echoed eerily across the plains as, in unison, twenty-two bullets bore into Ngum's back.

The Zulu chief's hold relaxed and he fell into the dust with his hostage. Even before they touched him, the traders knew their friend was dead. As they lifted him off the slain Zulu, Zara made for her lover's body but was caught halfway there and dragged back to the line of captive warriors.

'Just one moment of goodbye,' she begged as they shackled her to the other prisoners. 'I can't leave him thus for the birds to bury him. Mercy! One word of goodbye!'

Her hands were bound firmly together behind her. The camp had been set on fire. Shots rang and whips whistled in the air as the order was given to move off.

The Spanish cargo boat, *El Condor*, left the South African coast on August 15th, 1898. Carrying in its hold a relatively small load of fifty Zulu men and women for sale, it was bound for the Canary Islands. However, stopping to pick up more African booty on the island of Fernando Po, it was intercepted by a British anti-slave ship policing the Gulf of Guinea.

After a short bloody battle, the Spanish desperadoes commanding the *El Condor* were overcome and forced to surrender their cargo, which was then deposited at the Basel mission on Ambas Bay Kamerun, there to await forwarding to the British Protectorate of Sierra Leone, where the Zulus would be freed and given a new nationality.

Unconscious, half-dead, her body infested with sores, Zara was carried with the ten other Zulu girls from the *El Condor* to the mission infirmary. While her companions responded to the care and treatment dispensed by the missionary workers, the seventeen year-old girl lay delirious in bed re-living the nightmare voyage she had just completed in the dank, airless hold of the *El Condor*.

Even after she had regained consciousness, the horrible world of that slave ship seemed more real to her than the new world she now found herself in. She heard still the clanging chains, the groans of men and women cooped up in what looked more like an animal cage than a place for humans. She could neither eat nor drink without being overcome by nausea. Even the smell of food caused her to gag. When the time came for the voyage to Sierra Leone, it was decided that Zara was unfit to travel.

One of the German missionaries' wives, Miriam Leitmeyer, English by birth, took the young waif under her wing. When it was discovered that Zara's sickness was caused by pregnancy, Mrs Leitmeyer moved the girl to her own home and installed her in one of the two one-room shacks provided to house the Leitmeyer house help.

The other shack was occupied by the missionary couple's houseboy, Jacob.

As Zara's pregnancy advanced and vomiting ceased, the English lady tirelessly fought to save the young girl from the acute depression that engulfed her. Language was a barrier that prevented Mrs Leitmeyer from questioning her protégée about her past but, as Zara began to learn few words of the widely-spoken pidgin English, Mrs Leitmeyer man-aged to infuse some enthusiasm for life into the lonely girl. Comforted by the thought that she was carrying Nguni's child, Zara told herself that it was worth living to see that child grow. While she mourned her lover, she clearly saw that she would not want to return to Zululand even if that were possible. Nguni was no more, and without him, his people would not be able to withstand the onslaught by the land-hungry white settlers.

For a while, the dream of finding a new home, after losing her native land to Portuguese marauders, had almost come true. Now she was convinced her lot was to wonder the earth till the day she died. It was nothing to cry about. Her Zulu companions' from the slave ship had been carried off to some unknown country called Sierra Leone. They, too, would never see their homeland again. The old days when the black man controlled his destiny were gone - lost forever. The white man ruled the earth. The sooner she accepted that fact the better for her and the child she would soon bear.

Lost as she was most of the time in her dark thoughts, Zara could not help being fascinated by the missionary work going on around her. She was
deeply affected by the obvious disinterestedness of the missionaries. Far from being exploited, the Africans in and around the mission were the objects of the missionaries' solicitude. She soon learned that Hitside the mission, there were other white people not concerned with missionary work. The Germans, Zara was told, owned this country, ney had taken over from English traders and missionaries

and built roads, railways and big, beautiful houses. They hunted, planted and traded on a colossal scale, thanks to the inexhaustible source of free (black labour to be found in the country.

When her child was finally born on February fifteenth, 1899, Zara was disappointed. She had wanted a boy, a little Nguni whom she had imagined growing up to look just like his father.

But Miriam Leitmeyer was ecstatic. 'What shall we call the little angel?' she asked the new mother.

'I have no idea.' Why not Miriam? Zara thought and asked the white woman so.

The Englishwoman was delighted, 'I'll be her godmother, with your permission, of course. And I hope you'll share the little darling with me, Zara. Isn't it wonderful to have a young one around the house? And so pretty already. She's going to look just like you, Zara.'

Zara nodded but her smile was wistful. Nguni had disappeared forever. No image of him remained to walk this earth, gladdening some lonely mother's heart.

As the young lieutenant came riding up to the von Morgen mansion at ten o'clock that summer night, he was greeted by blazing lights, elegant horse-drawn carriages parked on the lawns, orchestral music floating out into the gardens, cultured voices raised in laughter and conversa-tion. He avoided the driveway and followed a side path to the back of the house passing, as he did so, the hall windows through which he could see the bobbing heads of several couples in dancing.

Samba knocked loudly on the kitchen door. It was opened im-mediately by Martha who stood for a moment dumbfounded at the sight of the soldier on the threshold. Then she gave a little shriek, 'But it's Herr Samba! Oh, my, you do look so different.' She didn't know what to do, how to greet him.

As the other servants in the kitchen gathered round the doorway, Samba took Martha by the shoulders and planted a kiss on each side of her face. 'Do I look so awful, Martha?'

'Awful, Herr Samba?' cried the maid. 'You look, you look . . . .? Martha looked about to swoon. 'Oh, just wait till Miss Sonia sees you. The master is giving a party for her today.'

Just then Myra von Morgen came in calling for Fritz. She stopped dead in her tracks at the sight of the imposing army officer towering over the heads of the kitchen staff. The young lieutenant took off his cap and advanced towards the elderly lady.

Samba held out his hand, 'Good evening, Fraulem.' There was a twinkle in the deep-set eyes that looked down into Myra's face.

'Heaven bless me.' breathed the old lady. 'If it isn't our very own Martin-Paul. She gathered the young man to her accommodating bosom then stepped back to admire him. 'My, my, my don't you look grand!'

Samba put his cap back on and grinned, Tin glad you think so, Ma'am.'

'Think so? Go on with you. You know you look uncommonly dashing. You're now a lieutenant in the Imperial Army, I see. I can tell. I once had a brother in the army. Are you coming in to join the party? It's for Sonia and Hans von Schlesser. They got engaged today.'

T must beg to be excused, Fraulein.' replied Samba. 'I've been riding all day and I'm fatigued. I'll just sneak into my rooms, if I may, and get some rest.'

Myra nodded, 'I understand. Martha will prepare your bath and bring you in a meal. Sonia will be so disappointed, though, that you can't even make an appearance.'

'You need not let her know that I'm here until the morning, Fraulein.'

'What an idea?' exclaimed the lady going out. 'Of course, I'll tell her and my brother that you've come.'

He had just gone into the bedroom and taken-off his cap when he heard the door to his apartments open.

'Is that you Martha?' he called, thinking it was the maid come in to prepare his bath.

Getting no answer he turned away from the bedside and saw Sonia standing in the bedroom doorway. She was dressed in a white sleeveless ball gown. Long white gloves covered her arms up past the elbows. She was carrying a gem-studded fan. On her golden head sat a diamond-embossed tiara. She was breath-takingly beautiful and carried herself regally.

'Hello, Princess,' Samba greeted her from the bedside.

Sonia gave a stifled cry and ran into his arms flinging her fan on the carpet. As he pressed her soft form to his hard chest Samba realized the girl he had said goodbye to just three years ago had turned into a woman. His companion of six years had been replaced by a full-fledged beauty, even more alluring than the one whose portrait he had admired in von Morgen's gallery years ago.

She seemed not to want to let him go. She took his face in her hands and examined it seriously. She ran her fingers over the bushy eyebrows and the short-cropped kinky hair.

'God you're beautiful!' she exclaimed earnestly.

Samba gave a short laugh and held her wrists imprisoned in his hands. His eyes were impenetrable, two dark pools contrasting sharply with her clear sea-green eyes that seemed to be devouring him. 'Congratula-tions,' he said softly. 'I hear you just got engaged.'

She turned away from him and sat on the bed. 'Yes, Papa is very happy, Hans is the nephew of the former Chancellor, von Bismarck.'

There was a knock on the door. Von Morgen came in holding out his hands in welcome. 'My son!' he called out to Samba. The old man was looking sprightly and happy.

Samba turned in his saddle as Sonia came galloping up, 'You're out of practice, Fraulein von Morgen,' he teased. 'What's happened? Too many parties and balls for you to be able to devote much time anymore to riding?'

Sonia made a face, 'You know that's not true. I can see the glowing reports Papa was getting about you from Cologne were not exagger-ated. I'm simply no match for you now.'

They tethered horses and strolled hand in hand to a remembered tree trunk from their teenage days and sat down, leaning their backs against the tree.

Samba brought out a small flask of tea from his hip pocket, poured out a cup for Sonia and drank from the mouth of the flask himself.

'Do you hear from your friend and his cousin?' asked the girl.

'Ndumbe and Felix? Yes. We write to each other regularly.'

'Has Rudolph taken over the throne yet?'

'Not yet. His father's old but still alive.'

'So what's he doing with himself?'

'He's joined the German civil service in Kamerun.'

'You remember that girl who was so crazy about him?'

'Can I ever forget? Whatever happened to her?'

'You won't believe this, but, Rudolph left without informing her. She almost went out of her mind until she received a letter from him six months after his departure.'

'What did he have to say?'

Sonia chortled, 'You know Rudolph. He said his father was old and sick and they were expecting him to die any time soon. He said as soon as his father was gone and he was king, he was going to change things in Kamerun so she could come and be his one and only wife. She showed me the letter. It was full of passion and verbal tears. At the end he said, 'Wait for me, my love. Do not get impatient. As soon as things are ready over here, I shall come for you.' But I suppose she got tired of waiting because, just last year, she got married to a lawyer from Munich.'

Samba shook his head. 'He never mentioned her in his letters, so I thought it best to stay clear of the subject.'

'What about his gentle cousin? Sonia wanted to know. 'What's become of him?'

'The last time I heard from him, he was thinking of going to Senegal for medical studies. He wants to become a doctor.'

'Rudolph's alter ego. He was such a sweet young man. For all Rudolph's brashness, it was amazing the influence his cousin had on him. I miss them both. I really do.'

They were silent for a moment, lost in reminiscences.

I shall be leaving in two days to join my regiment.' Samba broke the silence.

'What? So soon? After only a week?' Sonia turned to him, discon-certed.

The unfathomable eyes smiled down at her, 'A week is all we get. Then everybody has to report to his regiment for a year of service.'

'And after that?'

'After that, I shall come back here to wish both you and Germany goodbye. If you're still here. By the way, when's the wedding?'

She ignored his question and asked instead, 'Where are they sending you?'

'The fifty-fourth cavalry in Berlin.'

'But that's so-o far away, Martin-Paul!'

Samba threw back his head and laughed, 'For a moment there you sounded just like the fifteen year-old Sonia I met here seven years ago. Are you going to miss me now? After being used to my absence for the past three years, Sonia?'

She would not respond to his bantering tone but sat playing with her riding crop.

'Sonia?'

When she looked at him there were tears in her eyes.

'Martin-Paul?'

73

'Yes, Sonia?'

'There has never been any pretence between us from the day we first met. I want to tell you something.'

'Go ahead!'

'I've made a mistake. I should never have accepted Hans von Schlesser's hand in marriage.' The tears spilled over and rolled down Sonia's cheeks.

Samba smoothed them away with gentle fingers and took the girl's hand in his 'What has happened to change your mind so soon, Sonia?'

'I've seen you again.' She answered simply.

Samba was squeezing her hands, kneading them gently in his. He looked at those pink lips that were trembling as she looked hungrily up at him. And yet he would not kiss them.

'You love me.' He stated, savouring the moment.

She nodded, unable to speak at first. Then, 'I've loved you from the day we first met, only I didn't know it. I thought you were just a brother to me. I know now that it is more than that.'

It was now Samba's turn to be too moved to speak. He sat pressing Sonia's hands foolishly while he tried to formulate something coherent to say. But he could come up with nothing. He seemed to be drowning in the sea of her beautiful eyes.

Then Sonia said, 'Kiss me, Martin-Paul, Please.'

After that, he was able to talk. 'I stayed away for three years purposely, hoping that by the end of that time you would have missed me unbearably. It almost turned out to be a monumental mistake. I might have come back here and found you married.'

Sonia was pensive, 'I don't know how Papa is going to take this. He has his heart all set on this alliance with the von Schlesser's.'

But Samba was optimistic, 'From what I know of your father, I don't think he can have anything against you marrying me. We'll go to him together and tell him that we love each other.'

She would not accept that, 'I'd rather do it alone for now if you please, Martin-Paul. Don't forget there's still the engagement to be broken off. If you don't mind, darling, I'd rather we carried on for the next two days as if nothing has changed. After you've gone, I'll break the news to Papa and Hans in my own way. Please. Breaking off an engagement is not an easy matter, and there's a side of my father that you've never seen.'

'And there's a side of him you've never seen either. But I don't mind doing it your way if you feel it's best. Your father and I can always talk later.'

She hugged him fiercely, 'You're a treasure.'

A year later, Martin-Paul Samba was on his way back to Kamerun after an absence of nine years. Von Morgen had not opposed his daughter's preference for Samba over Hans von Schlesser. The old man had merely advised Samba to return home first and take a year to make preparations for receiving his future bride. The impatient Sonia "would not hear of being separated from the man she loved for so long. But Samba persuaded her to stay behind. Besides preparing for her arrival in Kamerun, the young man told her there were one or two scores he had to settle with some of his countrymen and, frankly, Samba preferred to have that matter over and done with before bringing Sonia in. When she insisted on knowing what the score was, he told her of the murder of his father and how he had decided on a military career as the easiest means of getting back at the perpetrators of the crime. The two lovers said goodbye therefore, and promised to write to each other every day.

Chapter Three

As she entered the gate leading to the Leitmeyers' compound, Zara smiled at her five year-old daughter's sing-song voice reaching her from Mrs Leitmeyer's living-room.

'...Up above the world so high. Like a diamond in the sty!' 'Not "sty" Miriam,' came Mrs Leitmeyer's voice. 'Not "sty"'.

'"Sky", the sky!'

'Sty!' repeated Miriam.

'No, no Sky! Look, up, up there. What's that?'

'Heaven'

Mrs Leitmeyer's deep voice rose in laughter. 'Okay. Heaven is up there. But what we see when we look up is the sky. See all those clouds floating? They are floating in the sky. That's the sky.'

'Does God live in the .sky Godmother?'

'God is everywhere, dear heart.'

'Mr Ndeley told us in Sunday school that God rose up into Heaven. He left his apostles and flew up into Heaven like a bird. So God is in the sty.'

'Sky!'

'Sky.'

Miriam Leitmeyer decided to let the matter rest for now.

"Is that you, Zara?' she called as Zara passed a window on her way to her cabin.

Zara stopped. 'It's me, Madam.'

'Come in here a minute will you?'

Miriam ran into Zara's arms as her mother stepped into the living-room. 'Hoo-hoo,' Zara whooped, throwing her daughter up in the air and catching her in her descent. 'I hope you haven't been a nuisance to your Godmother today. You know you mustn't tire her.'

'I haven't been any trouble, I swear it. Ask Godmother.'

Mrs Leitmeyer covered her ears with her palms in mock horror.

'Tsk, tsk, tsk,' disapproved Miriam's mother. I'm sure your Sunday school teacher told you little girls shouldn't swear.'

'All the children in school swear,' replied the child. 'If you don't say "I swear to God" then in means you're lying.'

Zara put her daughter down, 'Don't worry Madam, she'll learn as she gets older.'

Miriam Leitmeyer smiled indulgently at the two of them, 'Run along to the kitchen, Miriam, and ask Jacob, nicely, for a piece of cake. Then you can go out and play with your friends. Your mother and I have something to say to each other.'

Miriam skipped off, 'Oye-e! Thank you Godmother. Mr Jacob!' she called as she opened the kitchen door.

Mrs Leitmeyer's eyes misted over as the door closed behind the little girl. 'I shall miss that child,' she told Zara.

Picking up her cane, she moved from her armchair to the sofa, walking with a strong limp, dragging her right leg with the aid of her stick.

'The leg's getting no better' she announced sitting down heavily.

For the past year she had been suffering from sciatica which prevented her from moving around much. All her duties at the infirmary were now delegated to Zara who, surprisingly, in spite of her lack of education, had turned out to be a most capable administrator. The twenty-three year-old woman now managed the infirmary as if she had been groomed for the job.

She had learned how to deal with all routine ailments - malaria, children's illnesses, wounds, pregnancy; and she was a fine midwife. Above all, she ran the infirmary with an iron hand, whipping up a level of efficiency in the African workers which even Mrs Leitmeyer herself had never been able to achieve. Mrs Leitmeyer's esteem for her was immeasurable. Ah, what a girl such as Zara could have done for her people if she had been able to undergo formal training. With help from the primary school teacher, she had taught herself to read and write at home. Even now that she had attained a certain level of literacy, she was not satisfied. Zara was an avid student and now that Mrs Leitmeyer's outings were curtailed, the Englishwoman gave her all the help she needed in her studies.

But Miriam Leitmeyer never stopped deploring the fact that Zara had no social life of her own. Pretty as she was, she lived like a recluse and took no interest in men. Hardly anybody ever saw her out of her strict hospital uniform. Clothes and baubles held no attraction for her. The only concession she seemed to have made coquetry was to have kept her

hair in plaits for the past five years so that it now fell to her shoulders in a (thick heavy mass when she took it down. But nobody ever saw Zara's hair loose. She wore it in two thick braids close to her head, the better to carry her nurse's cap. Still, nothing could hide the magnificent figure beneath that stiff shapeless khaki uniform. Few were the men who passed by Zara without turning round for a second look.

Mrs Leitmeyer patted the empty sofa seat at her side. 'Sit down dear, and tell me what you have decided.'

Zara sat down and said shortly, 'I'll go.'

'Good girl,' approved the old lady. 'The Lord couldn't have chosen a better husband than Felix for you, Zara. Educated, a Christian, and 'from one of the best families. On top of that he's so handsome and good. What more could you ask for?'

'He's different from anything I've ever known,' replied the girl. 'I know. You once loved Miriam's father. But that was a long time ago. You're a different person from the girl who lived and fought alongside the Zulus. Nothing, nothing can ever bring back those times, and you owe it to your daughter if not to yourself, to provide her with a father and a name. What better name could you ally yourself with than that of the Douala royal family?'

Zara was not blind to the advantages that marriage with Felix Bele I would bring her. Her daughter would grow up among the country's elite and she herself would find a niche, perhaps a final harbour after her | wanderings.

'This is no life for you,' continued Mrs Leitmeyer. 'My husband and I must return home one day, and who can say what will become of you after we're gone?'

It had all started two years ago when a group of German and Douala officials from across the Mungo made an inspection tour of the Victoria Basel mission. In the group was Felix Bele, nephew of Chief Manga Bell of Douala, and a graduate from the William Ponty medical school in Senegal. The young man had promptly lost his head over Zara, and had spent the past two years pursuing the girl with unflagging determina-tion. Won over by the young man's patent sincerity and spurred on by Mrs Leitmeyer, Zara had started going out with Felix in the last year. Being unused to the worldly ways of this new breed of educated Kamerunians from the other side of the Kamerun river, Zara was wary. But Felix remained undaunted. He declared his intention of marrying her and had now invited her to Douala to meet his family.

Zara had hesitated, asking for time to think it out. Mrs Leitmeyer, meanwhile, was completely taken by Felix and had spared no pains in furthering the doctor's cause. She would not let Zara send the young man packing - Felix would make a perfect husband. Zara finally decided to make the trip to Douala and see the kind of life Felix was offering her.

'You'll probably be gone for at least a month' opinioned Mrs Leitmeyer. 'The first thing we have to do is to fit you out with a new wardrobe for your stay there.'

As Zara started protesting, the old lady held up her hand. 'The Manga Bells are not just anybody you know. They're royalty. You'll also discover that the Africans in Douala are much more sophisticated than their brothers here in Victoria. Believe me, you have nothing suitable to wear. Let me guide you.'

Zara bowed her head in submission.

After two days of donkey riding Zara and Felix arrived at the village of Etam.

'Are we going to cross over in that? Zara asked, pointing to the ferry bobbing gently on the lazy river before them.

'Right,' Felix descended from his donkey to a stunted guava tree.

She stood up, 'How far is Douala from the other bank?'

'Another three days journey.'

'What?'!'

Felix was amused at her obvious incredulity.

'You mean it's going to take a whole week to get there?'

'If there were a- similar ferry service farther up the Mungo, the journey would take half that time. We would have gone through Tiko and Mondoni in one day and then crossed over this same river at Mungo village before doing just one more day of riding to Douala. But, as you know, or your probably don't know, ignorant Zara, the whole of that area is nothing but jungle. That's why we had to come all the way to Kumba, Laduma, and now Etam, where we will cross over then start travelling almost back to a few miles from where we started. There is talk, though, of rubber and palm oil plantations to be opened by the Germans at Miselele and Mondoni. When that happens, a means of transporting the produce across the river will have to be found. If they don't build a bridge at Mungo, they will at least set up a ferry similar to this one.'

'And you've made this long journey each time just to come and see me?'

The young man's boyishly open face beamed at her. 'What's the journey compared to the joy of being with you, Zara?' He laid a hand against her warm cheek. 'I would cross ten mountains and twenty oceans just to see your beautiful face.'

The simplicity and directness of his sentiments filled her with a strange humility. This sweet handsome man expressed his feelings with a childlike straightforwardness that touched her in obscure recesses of her being. He'll be good to me thought Zara, and that is all that really matters.

And yet, and yet, why did the thought of Nguni keep intruding to fill her with such wistfulness? Would she never cease to long for him, that thunderous love of a life now dead and buried somewhere deep in her soul? Felix was an angel. His beautiful soul was reflected in his face. To be loved by him was to come in contact with all that was good and untainted in this life. She did not turn away from his gentle touch as he ran his fingers over her hair, now held together in one thick braid that hung down the back of her neck. Gone was the nurse's cap, the stiff khaki uniform. The Zara that stood before Felix dressed in a sleeveless pink shirt-blouse and full gathered calf-length skirt was a revelation to him. Never, not even in his wildest dreams, had he ever conjured up such a picture of physical perfection. He was now so desperately in love that it seemed to him he had had no life before meeting her.

The ferry, a simple affair of planks nailed together to form a flat surface about eight metres by ten, was slowly being rowed by its four member crew towards the couple. About one-quarter the area of the platform had been used to erect a simple shade consisting of a wide sheet of green tarpaulin held up by four wooden poles. Under this shade stood an important-looking person who, Felix ..informed

Zara, was the caption of the vessel. The captain's starched white khaki uniform shone brightly against his smooth black face, his cap planted firmly on the crown of his head. Felix and Zara led their donkeys onto the ferry and the four rowers started moving in unison, rowing to the other bank once again. Felix paid the captain for their tickets and they stood beside him under the shade for the duration of the crossing.

They spent three more days on the road as Felix had predicted, sleeping in village inns at night. On the morning of the fourth day, they reached Bonaberi and got off their donkeys to cross over the bridge which was built on an estuary. Half way across the bridge they stopped to look down into the water where fishermen were busy casting their nets.

'This is the river Wouri,' said Felix, 'after which Kamerun was named.'

'How do you mean?' asked Zara, mystified.

'The river' explained Felix, 'is full of prawns. When the Portuguese first got here long, long ago, even before the British, the French or the Germans, they called the river *"Rio dos Camaroes"* which simply means "River of Prawns." The Spaniards called it Camarones and today, the Germans call it Kamerun.'

Across the bridge lay Douala, a town as different from the village of Victoria as Mrs Leitmeyer had warned Zara. There seemed to be scores more white people here than at Ambas Bay. The town was huge. Here blacks and whites alike, lived in fabulous homes. The blacks here were all dressed in European clothes. There were so many people, nobody had time to wish a fellow passerby good morning. White men strolled about the streets with black girls at their sides, obviously not in a master-servant relationship. Zara gaped at a couple of banana-coloured indi-viduals who, Felix informed her, were the offspring of black-white couples.

The streets were wide, clean and paved. They rode round the busy metropolis to the seaport teeming with sailors, soldiers, traders and carriers. Big cargo boats were in the process of being unloaded while others were being loaded. And the carriers stood in long lines waiting to be hired to transport goods as far away as Ndjamena, or as near as a warehouse on the next street. German navy vessels also stood in the harbour, for the Kamerun coast was jealously guarded against rival colonialist-minded Europeans.

The two travellers stopped at market corners to watch the frantic haggling that went on between traders and their customers, Zara was astounded at the variety of European wares on sale - shoes, umbrellas, hats, attractively-printed fabrics, books, mirrors - there was everything in Douala.

As they turned to direct their donkeys' steps away from one such market scene, a male voice called out to Felix from behind them. They looked back to see a smartly-dressed man of about Felix's age smiling lazily as he sauntered up to them.

'The very person I wanted you to meet first!' exclaimed Felix dismounting, Zara following suit.

'Well, you obstinate devil,' called the stranger drawing up. 'So you finally got her to come!'

'Zara,' said Felix. 'Meet my cousin and best friend, Prince Rudolph Douala Manga Bell, heir to the Douala throne.'

The prince swept off his Stetson hat and bowed in salute before the smiling Zara, who soon found herself giggling as Rudolph took her proffered hand brought it to his lips instead of shaking it as she had intended.

Felix gave his cousin a savage dig in the ribs, 'Shove off you clown, you never know when to be serious.'

'Oh yes I do!' retorted Rudolph. Then to Zara, 'Believe me, Madam, this is no play-acting.' His reckless eyes swept over her. 'Tribute must be given where it is due, and beauty such as yours cannot pass unacknowledged.' He grabbed one hand of Felix's and one of hers and brought them together. 'Madam, accept my brother's hand in marriage. The royal family would be greatly honoured by your inclusion in their ranks.'

Zara's heart warmed to him. 'It is I who am honoured, your Highness,' she replied.

Rudolph clapped both hands over his ears, 'Now, hold it, hold it, Let's get this right straight away. There shall be no stiffness between the three of us. See this fellow here?' he flung an affectionate arm around Felix's shoulders. 'He and I have been like this from the beginning of time. I won't have his wife standing on ceremony with me. Felix here calls me Ndumbe, and that's what you'll have to call me too if we're to become friends. How's that lovely - Zara is it? Now let's go and meet the rest of the clan.'

But warm as Rudoph's welcome to Zara had been, it was an exception. The rest of the Manga Bell clan were not happy with Felix's choice of a bride, and had been set against her even before they saw her. There were several factors that disqualified Zara as a suitable wife for the doctor in the eyes of the Douala people. She was not of Douala origin - she was not even a Kamerunian. Nobody knew where she had come from. To most of the members of the Bell family, who had amassed their enormous wealth as middlemen in the now abolished slave trade, the fact that Zara had been rescued from a slave ship relegated her to a position of unspeakable inferiority. On top of all this, Zara was already a mother. A young educated man of Felix's status was supposed to return home after his studies and, with the judicious guidance of his family, choose an untouched girl, preferably from one of the other elite families of Douala. Nobody denied Zara's beauty but, they all agreed, Felix could very well make her his without having to marry her.

'Bring the girl over here to Douala if you want,' advised Felix's rather. 'Build her a house and spend all your time in her company if you wish. But don't marry her. You don't need to. We have already paid dowry on Eyumc Betote's daughter for you. Her father is an influential member of the Akwa clan and their union with the Bell family would consolidate our alliance with them against the Prisos. How shall I ever explain it to them if you refuse their daughter after your marriage with her has already been agreed upon?'

But Felix, who had been studying in Senegal when all these marriage arrangements were being made, offered to reimburse his father for the dowry he had paid to Eyume Betote, a suggestion which only angered his father further. Threatening his first-born with disinheritance, the old man warned him that Rudolph's father, Manga Ndumbe, would banish the young doctor from his realm if he went ahead with his disgraceful scheme of marrying an ex-slave. In silence Felix prepared himself for this eventuality, announcing to his cousin that he was ready to live in exile among the Bakweris on Ambas Bay with his Zara.

Meanwhile Zara returned to Victoria, smarting from the cold recep-tion the Manga Bells had given her. Apart from Rudolph's wife, Kwedi, no other woman in the family had looked on her kindly. Felix's sister, Charlotte-Amelia, made herself particularly obnoxious by making constant references to what she supposed must have been Zara's experiences on the slave ship she had been rescued from, She also kept asking Zara how many children she had. In apologising for his family's churlish behaviour, Felix explained that Charlotte-Amelia was the best friend of Ndedi Betote, the girl Felix was supposed to have married. 'It isn't strange therefore, that my sister should dislike you,' he said. But, insisted Felix, his family's dislike was something temporary. It would disappear with time. 'They cannot go on hating my wife forever, unless they want to turn me against them too;' added Felix.

Nevertheless Zara was mortified and told Mrs Leitmeyer that she could not see herself living in the midst of people who were so much against her. When Felix next came to see her, she told the doctor she had no wish to marry him. Felix remained understanding and undiscouraged, repeating only that his family had no say in his marriage. When Zara remained adamant, he offered to solve the problem once and for all by leaving Douala for good and coming to live in Victoria. 'It would cause me no pain, believe me,' he told Zara. And Zara believed him, but she would not hear of him breaking up with his family because of her.

'If you leave your people, I shall refuse to see you ever again,' she warned the doctor. 'Then make up your mind to marry me, Zara, because I shall never give you up,' answered Felix. For two years the wrangling went on without any solution being arrived at.

Fortunately, Felix had a formidable ally in Rudolf. When, in 1908, Chief Manga died, Rudolph acceded to the Douala throne and gave his royal approval to the union. The new chief followed his cousin to Victoria and together with Mrs Leitmeyer, the three of them persuaded Zara to accept Felix's hand. So in 1908, Felix and Zara were finally joined in holy matrimony at Pastor Lotin Same's Native Baptist Church in Bell-Town Douala. It was a sumptuous affair in which the groom's father refused to participate, predicting nothing but disaster for a union that was being made without his blessing. But Rudolph, the new head of the family, had given his seal of approval and there was nothing that Pa Bell could do. Zara said goodbye to her mentor, Miriam Leitmeyer, and brought her seven year-old daughter with her to Felix's home.

One year after the wedding, on April twenty-sixth, Mount Kamerun erupted, causing considerable damage to German possessions in Buea and on Ambas Bay. The ruling Governor at the time Dr Theodor Seitz, decided to move his government from Buea to Douala. Rudolph Manga Bell gave Seitz land on which to build his new headquarters. The Governor was a humanitarian administrator and soon became good friends with the Douala chief.

In Rudolph's palace, many an evening was spent discussing the German presence in Kamerun. Very often, the argument between the Kamerunians themselves became heated as they reviewed their recent history.

'The British would have given us a better deal had we stayed with them,' opinioned a young civil servant at dinner one evening.

'It would have been the lesser of two evils,' Felix agreed.

'You seem to have forgotten,' Rudolph intervened from the head of the table. 'That it was the British who failed to stick with us. When the Douala people, in 1881, realised that they could not avoid European take-over, my father wrote to Hewett, requesting British protection and annexation. Hewett took his time and only got round to us again after we had been obliged to sign the Protectorate treaty with Woer-mann.'

Felix chortled, 'The people dubbed him Too-late-Hewett because he arrived Douala four days after the treaty had been signed and spent two frantic weeks shuttling from one Douala chief's palace to the other, trying to get them to revoke their agreement with the Germans.'

'Anything so foolhardy would have resulted in stiff reprisals from the Germans, and needless spilling of African blood,' added Rudolph. 'After all, it wasn't as if the British were going to free us from alien rule.'

Zara sat drinking it all in, her mind drawing parallels between the European penetration of Kamerun and that of her own country and Nguni's. The pattern never changed. Everywhere the white man went, he subdued the African with his superior weapons and then proceeded to take all he wanted from him. The only difference now was that the Europeans had decided that trade in human flesh was to be stopped, much to the regret of some Africans, she was sorry to admit. Was she not married to a family who had enriched themselves by selling their brothers?

The young civil servant was talking again, 'The Germans are not going to be content with the terms of that treaty. Mark my words, the time is not far when you, my Lord,' looking in Rudolph's direction. 'Shall be nothing but a puppet in their hands. A monarch without a kingdom.'

'What do you mean?' everybody challenged him.

Rudolph said from the head of the table, 'The Protectorate Treaty signed with Nachtigal and Woermann on behalf of the German Government stated clearly that Douala land was to remain within Douala hands. Are you insinuating that the German Government has designs on our land?'

The young man, a clerk at the Governor's office, smiled mysteriously 'You would do well, your Highness, to have a heart to heart talk with your good friend, Theodor Seitz.'

There was absolute silence as everyone stopped eating to gape at the young speaker.

It was Rudolph who broke the silence, 'Over my dead body,' he swore through clenched teeth. 'Over my dead body.'

Governor Theodor Seitz blinked through rimless eyeglasses at the Douala chief looking expectantly at him across the office desk. 'I'm afraid the rumours you've heard are true, Your Highness.'

'But, Goddammit Seitz,' Rudolph's fist hit the table top loudly. 'The German Government cannot do this to us - not after all the concessions we've made to them. What? Expropriate our land? Dispossess us? You just hate our guts don't you? The Douala people have been the biggest thorn in your white flesh ever since you annexed our country, haven't they? They are proud people. They are your commercial rivals. They refused to pay your taxes. They have consistently refused to work on your plantations; they have refused to become your beasts of burden. In short, they refute your assumption of racial superiority over them. So now you want to teach them a lesson, put them in their place, is that it?

'You know I am strongly opposed to my government's expropriation policies, Your Highness.'

'You better be, Seitz, you just better be, because the Douala people are not going to stand for any of your high-handed German ways of operating. Not an inch of Douala shall be ceded to you except on our terms and when we judge fit. We shall fight to the last man for our patrimony. You say you've been recalled to Germany. Well and good. Make it your business to feed some sense into the heads of your Kaiser and his Chancellor.'

Chapter Four

About the time Zara was being rescued from the *El Condor*, Martin-Paul Samba was engaged in military campaigns to 'pacify' the central and northern parts of the Kamerun Protectorate for the Germans. Upon arrival in Kamerun, the young lieutenant had promptly been made a captain in the German overseas army, his special mission being the pacification of recalcitrant tribes who still opposed German rule in Kamerun. The young captain took to his task with gusto, but only his widowed mother knew that, while being a tool in German hands, her son was also using his position in the German army to carry out a personal vendetta against the people who had killed his father a decade before.

Samba first set out against his own people, the Bulus, and in the name of the government, meted out death to his father's murderers in and around Ebolowa. Only after that had been done did the young man tell his mother about Sonia and her expected arrival. Mrs Samba, whom everybody now called Auntie Ekodi, was temporarily floored by the news. A white girl for a daughter-in-law? How would that work?

'She's not just any white girl, Mama,' said Samba. 'She's Mr Kurt's daughter. She's more like family already.' Auntie Ekodi was not so sure. A white wife! Her son! Well! Whatever her dear Martin-Paul thought was best for his happiness she was ready to accommodate with. She and her daughter moved from the main residence into a smaller cottage in the Samba compound, and started getting the big house ready for Sonia's coming while Samba continued his campaigns inland.

The stipulated year of separation for the two lovers came to an end and Martin-Paul stopped receiving letters from Sonia. He also stopped writing, though it did cross his mind that Sonia had not written to tell him expressly that she was leaving Germany on any particular date on any particular boat.

When he did not hear from her for three months however, he assumed that she was on her way to Kamerun. Six months passed, then a year. Samba became very worried and set off two letters to Soma in rapid succession. He got no reply. As his anxiety mounted, the Captain's forays into the hinterland became more frequent and more savage. He was merciless and the very mention of his name was often enough to subdue the most obstinate of tribes. The German Govern-ment plied him with decorations and praise. Nothing was too good for him. He was the Germans' golden-haired boy and a devil in the eyes of his countrymen.

By Christmas of 1899, Samba had written nineteen letters to Sonia and her father without receiving a single reply. He could not fool himself any longer. Something was seriously wrong.

'Do you think she might have changed her mind, my son?' suggested his mother fearfully.

'Sonia?' Samba's face grimaced in his hurt. 'She would have let me know. Whatever she may be, she's not a coward. No, it's not that. Something terrible has happened. I can sense it. Some accident, but not at sea or we would have heard of it.'

'What can we do then?' asked Auntie Ekodi.

Samba stood staring at his feet lost in thought. Finally he looked up and said, 'I'm going to Germany.'

'What? Leave us again?'

'That's the only way I can find out for certain. I even wrote to a friend of mine who was at the academy with me to find out for me what has happened to Sonia and her father. It's been four months now. I still haven't heard from him.'

'He might still write, my son'

'I'll give him between now and the time I'm actually ready to sail, which won't be before another month is out. If he still hasn't answered my letter by that time, I'll just go as planned.'

Within two weeks of this conversation, Martin-Paul received a reply from his former schoolmate which only made the captain more determined to go to Germany. According to the letter, Samba's friend had learnt that Sonia von Morgen was dead. The young man wrote that he had gone to the von Morgen's house and seen both the old man and her sister. But he had not been able to get any details concerning the girl's death. Not even the servants could be induced to release any information.

'I've got to find out,' Samba told his mother, his eyes burning. 'If she's dead why wasn't I told? And they've been sitting in that house all this time receiving my letters. Why has nobody answered them? I have to see von Morgen myself.'

Auntie Ekodi was afraid for her son, of what he might do once he got to Germany. She cautioned him to keep a cool head, 'Do not do anything rash, my child. Think of your poor mother and sister who shall be waiting for you to come back.'

'Don't worry, Mama.' Samba patted her hand absently. I'm only going to find out the truth I shall come back to you.'

Two days before he was due to sail, Samba received a second letter from his friend in Germany. A few days after sending off his last letter to Samba, the young man had run into a certain Frau Martha Mendel, a former maid at the von Morgen mansion who, when she found out that Samba's friend was making enquiries on behalf of Martin-Paul, im-mediately offered to give him the whole story. According to Martha, Kurt von Morgen had never wanted Samba for a son-in-law. He had pretended, however, to have nothing against the marriage just to get rid of Martin-Paul, and in the hope that by the end of a year's separation from Samba, Sonia's feelings would have changed. When, at the end of the year, Sonia still wanted nobody but her Kamerunian suitor, von Morgen was forced to take his stand.

A bitter quarrel ensued, and Sonia threatened to run away. It was then that von Morgen had her locked up in an asylum, promising to release her if she would give up the idea of marrying Samba. Within one year of living in the asylum Sonia von Morgen actually became mad and died by her own hand.

When he finished reading the letter, Samba *went* into his bedroom, shut and locked the door, then set about tearing it apart. Every single thing he could break with hand, he broke. What he could not break, he threw on the floor or at the wall, then trampled on it with all the strength in his body. All the while he was crying silently, a lion in its cage gone berserk. Auntie Ekodi and sixteen year-old Nadja knocked on the door and called out to him with no results. His mother decided not to ask for help. There was no need to advertise the fact that her son had gone temporarily mad. She sat down by the door and prayed and waited for the door to open.

Finally, after eight hours, the door opened. His mother and sister ran to embrace him but Samba drew back, only motioning for them to find seats for themselves. Auntie Ekodi found a broken suitcase and sat on it while Nadja sat on a pile of clothes. Samba sat on the steel edge of his upturned iron bed and gave them facts of the story. His eyes were bloodshot and perspiration stood on his forehead but he seemed calm.

I'm still going to Germany,' he told them.

'What for my son?' demanded Auntie Ekodi. 'There's nothing you can do now.'

'I'm going to kill him.' said Samba

'No!' breathed the two women

'Yes.' said Samba softly. 'I'm going to kill von Morgan.'

No amount of tears on his mother's part could dissuade him. He left for Ulm as planned.

By the time he returned from Germany a year later, his mother was a bundle of nerves and had already given him up for dead.

He smiled bleakly as she embraced him and told her, 'it's alright, Mama. It's all over. I've done it. Have no fear. No-one saw me in Ulm and they won't ever find his body.'

Auntie Ekodi could do nothing but cry. Her son had become so strange, so quiet. But he went about his work as before, although the pacification campaigns became less frequent. He started collecting arms and hiding them in his room.

One day he called his mother and said to her, 'Mama, I have been a fool all of my life. Sonia's death was a great blow to me. I don't know if I shall ever get over it. But over and above that, there is something else which has filled me with a bitter pain.'

'What is that, my son?'

'Has it ever occurred to you to ask why von Morgen preferred his daughter to die rather than have her marry me?'

'He could not have known that she would take her own life, Martin-Paul.'

'Oh yes he did, Mama. I have never told you but Sonia was a fragile person inside and her father knew it. When we first went to Germany, it was I who saved her from disaster and healed a big wound in her that had been inflicted on her by her father. I pulled her back from the abyss. The worst thing von Morgen could have done was to lock her up in an asylum for insane people. However, what I wanted to tell you is this: I have now realised just how much we meant to von Morgen. We didn't really mean much to him.

He could come here to Africa and live with my Aunt Katie and profess to love not only her but you and I and Papa. He called me his son, but when that love was put to the test, it failed to stand up. Do you understand what I'm telling you Mama?'

'I think so my son. Massa Kurt never saw you as someone fit to marry his child.'

'Why, Mama?'

'Because you're a black man, my son. It was presumptuous of us to imagine that Massa Kurt ever saw us as his equals.'

Samba smiled at his mother, 'Mama, you're being kind to me. I know I am the only one who made that mistake. I know you and Papa never presumed any such thing. It was Martin-Paul the educated, the learned one, who failed to see the simple truth you never lost sight of.'

Auntie Ekodi squeezed her hands together and looked down in anguish, 'They're white people, my son. They can never love us. But that should not pain us. We don't need their love to be happy, and whatever they may think of themselves, we know they aren't better than us.'

'Wise words from an intelligent, uneducated woman. Mama, all these things you're telling me, I realise them now. But only now. It has taken me a whole lifetime to realise them. Meanwhile I have turned my own people against me. I have made myself the white man's tool. I want to change that, Mama. I want the white man out of Kamerun. I want to wipe that smile of superiority from their hypocritical faces.'

'It is too late now my son. They need us too much and we have become dependent on them. They won't let us go.'

Samba looked at his little mother his eyes glowing with wonder. 'How well you put it, Mama. I would never have believed you thought of such things. You're very right. But there's one thing I want to do first. I want to re-instate myself in the eyes of my countrymen as a true Kamerunian. From now on I shall be working against the Germans.'

'Be careful, my son.'

'I shall be very careful. I still need them. You see these weapons I've started accumulating? I need much, much more. My expeditions shall still continue, for that's the easiest way for me to take their arms without arousing suspicion.'

It was uphill work for Martin-Paul Samba but he managed, after ten years, to convince his people that he was sincere in his change of heart. His campaigns into the hinterland now became the opportunity for him to embark on an energetic campaign to foment a revolt of the natives against German rule. So successful was he that when the Ebolowa throne became vacant in 1910, he resigned his commission in the German army and became traditional chief.

By this time his plan had crystallised in his mind. He was committed to ousting the Germans from Kamerun. An eloquent speaker, he stressed the merits of dealing with the Europeans on an equal footing rather than as their subjects. Britain, France and Germany were engaged in an unending squabble over Kamerun, and even though for now, the Germans were masters here, the other two colonial powers were waiting in the wings for an excuse to interfere in the German Protecto-rate.

Samba knew the Kamerunians by themselves could not shake off the Germans. His plan was a simple one: Pit the Europeans against each other. First of all, find a pretext for calling in Britain and France to 'save' the Kameruns from Germany. After the three powers would have fought each other for some time without either one succeeding in asserting herself as the victor, Kamerun would come up with the suggestion that the European powers forget the idea of annexing the country. The colony would ask for her sovereignty in return for leaving herself open for trade with the three contenders for her hand. In other words, Kamerun would become a prostitute for her own betterment. His plan was feasible, Samba stressed, if only Kamerunian chiefs would speak with one voice.

Thus his major mission was to get all the other traditional chiefs committed to his game plan. His friend Rudolph Douala Manga Bell did not refuse his support, but he remained sceptical. He did not hesitate to tell Samba that the plan was too simplistic, that it failed to take into account the inherent greediness of the Europeans.

None of the three powers involved would agree to share Kamerun's wealth with the others. Each power-struck nation was bent only on establishing her supremacy in whatever African territory attracted her interest. It was Rudolph's contention that even if they could evict the Germans, they would only be exchanging them for either a French or British yoke.

Samba continued to spirit away the German arms to Ebolowa. After his resignation, he started buying smuggled arms from the Belgian, British and French traders on the West African coast. He set up a military training ground in Biba just outside the town of Ebolowa where he himself trained young Kamerunians in sophisticated warfare. Keeping up with European politics with the help of his spies scattered throughout the German households and offices, the Ebolowa chief found more and more reason to be optimistic.

Europe was working itself up to a state of hysteria in an arms race that in Samba's opinion could only end in a general war. Germany was leading in this race, thereby causing fear in her neighbours and prompting them to isolate her. Even here in the colonies, frightened French and British officers were beginning to spread anti-German propaganda that could only be a reflection of the tension back home. Instances of German brutality and greed were quick to be pointed out and the Africans were urged to be ready to join hands with their European friends abroad in liberating the world from German tyr-anny.

Then the news broke out that Germany was casting covetous eyes on Douala territory namely, the Joss plateau. Using the Berlin Confer-ence as cover, the Germans affirmed that their stations on the Kamerun coast gave them a just claim to adjoining territories inland.

The kings of Douala rose in unison to point out that the Protectorate Treaty of 1884 carried no such clause. In fact, they said, the German claim was in contravention of the treaty. The Berlin conference, Kaiser Wilhelm replied, superseded any smaller treaties made at African national level. Berlin what? The Africans asked the Europeans. And what relevance could a conference held in Berlin without their know-ledge have on their domestic affairs?

And so on and on, with the Germans growing less and less diplomatic as they became more and more menacing. Samba knew at this point that he could count on the support of the Douala chiefs in his cherished plans for Kamerun - at least as far as evicting the Germans concerned. He began preparing for a trip to Douala.

'Baby, Baby, Baby, if you don't want me to, I won't go. You know it's as simple as that.' Felix knelt before his wife as she sat crying on the edge of the bed. His arms went round her waist and he rested his head lovingly on her swollen stomach for a second before looking up at her. 'Don't you want me to go? I've already half a mind to turn down this American scholarship, so torn up am I already at the idea of leaving you.'

Zara dried her eyes, 'Of course you must go. You wouldn't have started any of this if it didn't mean something to you.'

'It does mean a lot to me, Zara. Right now I'm very unsatisfied with the work I'm doing at the hospital. With all my big title of Doctor, I'm being used as nothing better than an infirmarian. I'm good only for bandaging wounds and dispensing prescribed medicines. The white doctors won't let me do any consultations. If I enter an operation room, it is only to perform the duties of a nurse. Do you wonder that I cringe each time someone calls me Doctor?'

Zara placed a hand on her husband's cheek, 'A man must feel confident of himself.'

'Exactly!' Felix got off his knees to sit by her. 'What I've decided to do is to leave the doctoring field to the Germans who are guarding it so jealously, and branch out into Pharmacy. When I come back from this three-year course, I shall be my own master. I plan to open my own Pharmacy and do my work as I judge best without having a bunch of superiors breathing down my neck.'

'It sounds wonderful,' enthused Zara. 'And I shouldn't be getting emotional about it. But it's going to be lonely here without you.'

Felix laid a hand on her belly, 'It's going to be lonely for me too. But you'll have Ndumbe and Kwedi. I'm leaving you in their care. You know they will guard you and the child, when it comes, with their lives.

Then there's Pastor Lotin who married us, and who's almost like a father to me. They'll take care of you for me.'

Zara started crying again. I'm afraid Felix. All this talk of the Germans wanting more land from Douala . . .'

Felix laughed, 'Is that what's worrying you, my Zara? You'll soon come to learn that squabbling with the Germans or the French or whoever has control over us at a given time, is our way of life here. When they push we also push and both sides end up making a few concessions. There's no cause for alarm. Rudolph will stand up to them and it shall come to nothing. You'll see.'

'I really do hope you're right, Felix.'

'I am. The Germans are masters here, but they've always known how to stay within certain bounds. They know and we know that they're stronger than us. But if it should boil down to a confrontation, they know we've got friends, and powerful ones too.' Felix shook his head. 'No, nothing will come of all this. Germany wouldn't make that mistake.'

Felix lifted his wife onto the big spring bed and lay next to her. He slid one strap of her loose cotton dress off her shoulder then the other. Her naked breasts throbbed with desire as he gently kneaded the swollen nipples. He gazed down at her and felt himself falling, falling into the fire of her smouldering eyes as they beckoned to him to love her..

Felix had to leave for the United States almost immediately but, before leaving, he removed his four months pregnant wife and her daughter from their apartments in his father's home and installed them in his cousin's palace. Eyes were raised and tongues clucked, but the doctor knew better than to leave Zara alone among his hostile family. Besides, Rudolph was as much his family as his parents were. Zara wept disconsolately when her husband left.

'I shall never see that man again,' she told Rudolph's wife.

Kwedi chided her gently, 'What a wet hen you've become with your pregnancy, Zara.'

'I feel it in my bones,' insisted Zara.

I know just how you feel,' her friend comforted her. 'I went through the same thing when Ndumbe left for studies in Ulm several years ago, although we weren't even married then. You'll be surprised how fast a year goes by. Before you know it, he'll have been gone two years and you'll be waiting for the third to come to an end. Meanwhile, your baby will be here soon to keep you occupied.'

Before the year was out, Rudolph Manga Bell was again facing the German governor across his office desk. This time the Douala chief had come in the company of Pastor Lotin Same.

The new Governor, Otto Gleim, two months old in Kamerun, cleared his throat. 'The decree you're holding in your hand just arrived from Berlin.'

Rudolph held up the paper in question and read out loud, 'Decision to move Natives from Douala to a New Location Separated from Europeans by one Kilometre. In order to prevent land speculation and also improve health conditions for Europeans, it has been decided. . .' Rudolph let the document flutter from his fingers to the floor, 'If living side by side with us natives is a health hazard for you,' said the chief softly, 'Why do you want to put only one kilometre between yourselves and us? Put a million kilometres, in fact leave Kamerun. What could be safer for your health than that?'

Otto Gleim refused to be ruffled by Rudolph's sarcasm. 'I can understand your bitterness, your Highness. Believe me, I am on your side. If there is anything I can do . . .'

'Have you done your best to dissuade your government from taking this action?' demanded Rudolph.

'I have done my best. I'm still doing all in my power. . .'

'Perhaps you have not been persuasive enough,' cut in Manga Bell. 'You haven't put our case forcefully enough.'

'The Governor looked pained,' I assure you. . .'

'I might have to send a representative to Berlin,' Rudolph interrupted again.

'By all means do,' agreed the Governor. 'It might convince you that I have been trying to move Heaven and Earth for you and your people.'

Rudolph was looking at the German official speculatively. 'If all else fails, there's one other thing that you could do for us.'

'What's that?'

'Give us guns,' said Rudolph.

Pastor Lotin stifled a gasp while the Governor's eyes almost turned in his head.

'That might turn out to be the only meaningful help you could possibly give us,' added Rudolph easily.

Otto Gleim looked thoroughly ill at ease. He looked to Lotin for help which the churchman was unable to give him.

'Really, my friends,' said the German clearing his throat. 'Let us hope that matters do not come to such a point.'

'And if they do?' challenged Rudolph.

It was the Governor's turn to look speculatively at his interlocutor, 'Are you trying to tell me that your people are prepared to take up arms if matters came to ahead?'

'You've read me right Gleim.' said Rudolph rising to his feet. 'You may tell your Kaiser that. I sent him the same message last year. There shall be bloodshed and not only Kamerunians are going to die. Kindly tell him that.'

As they descended the Governor's front steps, Rudolph and Lotin conferred with each other.

'A Ngondo must be convened before the end of the year, no later,' stressed the Pastor.

'Yes.' 'Samba must be invited.'

'You echo my thoughts, Pastor.'

The young man was very attractive and piqued Charlotte-Amelia's curiosity. Of medium build and height, he had an infectious smile and a debonair manner that marked him out as someone who had been abroad. As he told the Beles, Jim Akaku was only three months old in Kamerun after studying in the University of Iowa for the past four years. He was a native of Bafut in the Grasslands area of Kamerun and before going to U.S., he had been a student in King's College, Lagos. Felix Bele had come to Iowa in Jim's last year there and the two Kamerunians had naturally become friends. When Jim had expressed the strong desire to live in Douala after his return home, Felix had given the young graduate a letter of introduction to his parents asking his family to use their influence not only to find Jim a suitable house, but also to obtain a job for him in the civil service.

'You can put up with us until you find a place of your own,' offered Pa Bele. 'As for a job with the government, I'll take you to see my nephew, Rudolph, tomorrow. There should be no problem with that.'

'I'd also like to see Felix's wife.' said the young man. 'I have a parcel for her from Felix.' He had already distributed Felix's presents to his parents, brother and sister.

'Tell me,' said Ma Bele 'How's Felix doing?'

'He's doing fine, Ma,' answered Jim. 'He still has three more years of studies to complete.'

Ma Bele heaved a sigh, 'Such a long time. He seems to have spent all his life away, studying.'

'Felix says in his letter that you're married to an American girl,' said Charlotte- Amelia.

'That's right.'

'Is she white?'

'Nope. Black like you and I.'

'I wonder what they're like, those ex-slaves.' Charlotte-Amelia went on. She was already resenting this unknown black American who had got her hooks in such an attractive Kamerunian. Yet, it was this very fact that tripled James Akaku's value in Charlotte-Amelia's eyes. Marrying a black American was just as prestigious as marrying a white woman. It invested the husband with an aura of glamour. There must be something special about an African who could win the love of an American. Charlotte-Amelia looked at Jim Akaku with doubled in-terest. Could this man possibly shift Martin-Paul Samba from the place he had occupied in her heart all these years? She could tell that James Akaku was already smitten by her. It came as no surprise. Martin-Paul was the only man she knew who remained indifferent in the face of her beauty.

'When's your wife joining you?' enquired Ma Bele.

'As soon as I'm settled, I shall send for her.'

Charlotte-Amelia was pleased at Jim's answer. She had time to work on the American graduate and maybe even stop him from sending for his wife.

Chapter Five

S amba arrived at Douala late one hot Sunday afternoon after a three-day journey from Ebolowa. Passing unnoticed through the dusty streets and deserted market stalls, he was greeted by the peaceful sight of the semi-carnival atmosphere that characterised modern African Sundays - various societies and groups meeting to discuss important social or family matters in an ambience of merriment, feasting and dancing, While the Europeans spend the day quietly and the missionaries advocated prayer and reflection for the Lord's Day, the Africans, Christian and pagan alike, had invested Sunday with an aura of pageantry and festivity that smacked highly of primitive idolatry and fetish. Almost every street corner was the scene of native dancing and drumbeat - men and women of a clan, a church group or a secret sect, meeting to drink and be merry this one day of the week.

Passing a Roman Catholic church, Samba heard the *'O salutaris hostia'* of the beginning of Sunday Benediction. Here too, was another esoteric world, perhaps the biggest of them all. The Africans, with their predilection for animism, took to the statues, the incense, the ringing bells and aspersing with enthusiasm. . . *Unit Trmoque Domino Sit sempiterna gloria.'*

The Latin chant, by virtue of its incomprehensibility, held strong meaning for them. It was the abracadabra of the priest, magician and medium to this strange and fearful God who made the white man clever and the black man stupid.

Samba could imagine the scene at the altar at the moment - the incense swirling around the altar, the bells jingling, the white priest mumbling and invocating, the altar boys on their knees behind him, hands joined in prayer, their faces bent to the floor, swaying from side to side m a trance. Samba knew it all - he used to be a fervent altar boy himself.

The similarities between Catholic worship and indigenous African iconolatry had a common denominator somewhere, somehow ... He wished his limited learning could have permitted him to pierce the mystery.

His friend's palace was quiet and practically deserted.

Samba decided that the family must have been invited somewhere for one of the many Sunday gatherings. Passing the several cottages that constituted the palace, he headed for the main building, Rudolph's personal residence, where he could make out two female figures on the veranda - a woman sat on a rocking chair while a little girl combed the woman's hair. Probably Rudolph's wife (whom Samba had never met) and her daughter.

They both looked up curiously at him as he reached the front balustrade. Then the woman rose abruptly to her feet, her hands clutching her breast with a gasp, staring at him, fear in her eyes. As she tethered his horse to the railing and climbed the three steps to the porch, she swayed and placed a hand on the girl's shoulder to steady herself. Tall and dark, with the radiance of a full moon, Samba saw she was great with child, her striking wild - looking face framed by abundant curly hair that hung down to her shoulders.

He called out a greeting in Douala but only the girl answered. The woman continued to gawk at him as at an apparition. She addressed him but in a strange language, her breast heaving in obvious agitation. Samba felt his heart jump then settle down into his stomach. Her rich ripe body swollen in imminent motherhood sent the blood barraging through his veins in a tumult. Rudolph's wife, a voice said in his head, and carrying his child - you dare not look at her with such lustful eyes.

106

To cover his confusion, he began speaking once more in Douala, 'You must be Ndumbe's wife. Where . . .'

The girl cut him short, 'My mother does not speak Douala. You must speak in English.'

'Excuse me,' Samba said obeying the girl. 'But aren't you the wife of

Rudolph Manga Bell?' As far as he could recall, Rudolph had married a Douala girl.

'No,' answered the child as her mother remained mute.

'Then a thousand pardons for my mistake. Let me introduce myself. I am Ndumbe's friend, Martin-Paul Samba, chief of Ebolowa. Now may I ask who you are?'

'What?' breathed the woman. 'My God!' She collapsed unto her seat, a hand to her forehead, still staring at him. Her eyes shut for a moment then opened to look once more at the visitor. She took in his tall frame, the proud bearing, the deep-set eyes beneath the bushy eyebrows, the strong military figure. With a sigh she seemed to return to reality and stood up again, a disarming smile on her face as she extended a hand in greeting. 'Forgive a foolish pregnant woman, Your Highness. For a few moments there I thought I was seeing a ghost. Let me welcome you in the name of the family. I am Zara, Felix Bele's wife. Felix left us four months ago for studies in America. And this is my daughter, Miriam.'

While she spoke and he held her cool hand in his, unwilling to let it go, her words seemed to vibrate through his entire body. He gazed spellbound at her strange exciting features until she pulled her hand away to introduce her daughter. He wanted to talk a bit more, but she called for a servant to carry the visitor's bags into the house and prepare him a bath. Miriam was ordered to see to the lighting of the kerosene lamps. Zara invited Samba into the parlour explaining that the family had been invited to Deido for a death celebration but would all be back before it got too late.

Samba was at table having a meal when the Manga Bells got home. Recognising his guest from the door, Rudolph at once clicked his heels, giving a mock military salute.

Getting to his feet Samba barked out in German, 'Achtung!'

Down went Rudolph's hand as he executed.

'Officer,' bellowed Samba. 'Forward march!'

Rudolph started towards him with mincing steps, his hands held out daintily.

They collapsed into each other's arms, weak with laughter. Samba thumped his friend on the back, 'You haven't changed, you great monkey. I should have thought old age would have tamed you by now.'

'Oh, he gets worse with age,' said Rudolph's wife as she too entered the room, her two sons following her.

Samba hastened to shake her hand, 'You must be Ndumbe's wife,' he said for the second time that day. He turned to the two boys. 'Your sons, I take it?'

'Yes. Alexander and Frederick.'

Frederick, a boy of eleven and the younger of the two, bowed low before Samba as he shook his hand. 'We have heard a lot about you, Your Highness. I want you to know that my brother and I greatly admire the work you're doing and as soon as we're old enough, we're coming to join your army.' The boy stopped, out of breath, his eyes devouring Samba in obvious worship.

Samba patted the young man on the back and gave him a second handshake, 'That's it, my boy. We need all the help we can get. I'll be waiting for you when you're ready.'

'In another three years, Your Highness. I'll be almost fifteen then and strong enough.'

'Agreed. We shall be expecting you.'

A derisive snort from one of the doorways had all heads turning towards Miriam who advanced towards the boys saying, 'Nobody's going to let you give up your studies to join the army. He's just saying yes to please you.'

Frederick stuck his tongue out at her, 'What would you know about anything, Mbonga?' They called her Mbonga after the small bony fish that the Africans smoked and used in almost all their cooking. Miriam had earned this nickname on account of her tall bony build.

She crossed her arms and stood before Frederick, 'It takes men to fight a war, stupid, not soft boys of almost fifteen. Besides, Uncle Ndumbe would never, never let you and Alex give up school. Want to bet?' She held out her hand palm up for Frederick to seal the bet by striking it with his own palm.

'You haven't said hello to our guest, Miriam,' Kwedi interrupted.

'We've already met!' Miriam turned with a triumphant smile.' Ask him who served him his food.'

'Well. . .' Kwedi turned half-embarrassed, towards Samba.

'That's right,' Samba came to the rescue. 'The young lady and her mother have been taking care of me since my arrival.'

Frederick and Alexander snickered at the use of 'young lady' in reference to Miriam.

Miriam threw them a withering look, 'Boys!' Her tone was scathing. Turning back to Samba, 'Mama sent me to ask if you would like some corn beer with your meal.'

'We'll do even better than that,' cut in Rudolph. 'Ask Zara to join us. We're going to open a bottle of genuine Johnny Walker eh, Martin-Paul? I bet that sounds better than corn beer!'

The next afternoon, Samba had lunch at the Beles. Apart from Felix's parents, there was their son, fourteen year-old Jason-Kinge as well as Felix's twenty-six year-old sister, Charlotte-Amelia. After the meal, they sat on the veranda sipping corn beer while the family tried to catch up on news about Samba. Their guest, James Akaku, was out job-hunting with Rudolph.

'Still not married, Martin-Paul?' enquired Ma Bele, a small sad-faced woman who had once been a beauty.

'Not yet, Auntie.'

'What? Not even engaged?' put in her daughter. She was a slim light-skinned beauty with delicate features whom her parents were beginning to fear would never marry because she kept putting off suitor after suitor. It was an unspoken secret that Charlotte-Amelia was in love with Samba, and had been hoping for years that her brother's friend would pop the question. Her mother, who saw no future in the girl's infatuation, kept wishing that Samba would get married, thereby forcing Charlotte-Amelia to accept someone else.

Ma Bele sighed deeply, 'Young people today have no regard for tradition and convention. I don't know how you expect to carry on your lineage if you don't marry and have children.'

Samba smiled, 'You shouldn't complain too much, Auntie. At least Felix had done well for himself, and you're soon going to be grandpa-rents.'

Felix's father who had been silently smoking his tobacco pipe spat into the dust beyond the porch railings, 'Some daughter-in-law he has saddled us with. I shall never recover from the shame.'

Samba's eyebrows shot up, 'Zara? Why, she's a splendid woman!' A knowing smile played on the patriarch's lips while Charlotte-Amelia exclaimed in irritation, 'I can see you've fallen under her spell just like Ndumbe and Felix.' 'I swear that woman is a witch!'

Samba was shocked but concealed it, 'I don't know anything about her. I only saw her for a few minutes last night. Where's she from?'

'Nobody knows,' answered Ma Bele petulantly. 'Felix found her over at the Baptist mission in Victoria. He says she was taken off a slave ship.' 'Good God!' Samba was intrigued. Poor Zara. A fine welcome she must have received from her stuck-up in-laws. No wonder Felix had left her in Ndumbe's care. He wondered whose child the forward Miriam was - certainly not Felix's. Suddenly he felt an irrepressible urge to see Felix's wife again. He had. wandered round and round the palace all morning hoping to run into her, but she had not come out of her room by the time he left for his lunch date. He remembered the agitation his arrival had caused in her and wondered what lay behind it.

Samba stood up; 'I must leave you now. Ndumbe and I haven't talked yet. I suppose you all know about the crisis that has brought me here.'

Pa Bele nodded, 'All our hopes are in you young men. But you must proceed with care. The white man has a lot going for him.'

'Don't I know it!' agreed Samba. 'Well, be seeing you.'

As he went down the steps Jason-Kinge asked, 'Did you bring your guitar?'

'Sure did.'

'Great!' the boy called. I'll be over to take some lessons. You promised me last time.'

'Me too!' chirped in Charlotte-Amelia.

'You're both welcome.' Samba assured them.

She was sitting in a rocking chair on the back porch, swaying gently back and forth as she supervised the cooking of the evening meal by her daughter and a houseboy. The rocking stopped as she caught sight of him.

'Hello-Zara.'

'Your Highness.'

He drew up a stool and sat beside her, 'I hope you will imitate the rest of your family and call me Martin-Paul.'

She was gazing at him with eyes that had a faraway stricken look.

'Do I disturb you, Zara?'

'No, of course not.' She seemed to recall his presence.

111

'I remind you of someone,'

'Yes.'

'Does it make you sad?'

She looked at him, confused, while her expression changed from sad to gay and back to sad again.

Just then Miriam came up with a panful of egusi for her mother's inspection, 'Will this do Mama?' the girl curtsied in Samba's direction as she held out the ground pumpkin seeds for her mother's verdict.

'How many cups do you have here?' asked Zara, poking a finger in the white powder. 'Two.'

'Better add one more.' She resumed her rocking as Miriam dashed off to the kitchen with her pan of egusi.

Samba watched Felix's wife, spell-bound. "Everything about her seemed to fascinate him - her graceful hands, her long legs with the feet bare at this moment, her dark burnished skin, even the big swollen belly that was carrying Felix's child. . .

'Is Kwedi at home?' he asked, trying to make conversation.

'No, she left for Deido this morning to visit her sick mother. She'll be back tomorrow.'

Samba barely heard her. A treacherous thought was pounding

through his brain. Too bad, Felix. Too bad you're not here. I'm going

to steal her from you, I can't let her go.   '

That night, Rudolph, Samba and Pastor Lotin stayed up long after everyone else had gone to bed. A bottle of whisky between them, they sat round one end of the dining table, planning.

'Our best help,' said Samba. 'Would be a general war m Europe. At least a war involving Britain, France and Germany.'

'With Britain and France allied against Germany. How lucky can you get? And even if there's going to be such a war, how are you sure it's going to happen in time to be of any use to us?' This from Rudolph.

Samba cleared his throat, 'To answer your first question, I'm not counting on chance as much as you believe. First of all, don't forget that Britain and France, though traditional enemies, have been on friendly terms since 1904 when they signed their *Entente Cordiale*. Now, Germany is very disturbed by this friendship. In fact, she's downright scared - so scared she has been taking steps to break the Franco-British alliance.

'Fortunately for us, Germany's attempts have been spectacularly unsuccessful, so unsuccessful as to strengthen the very *Entente* she's trying to spoil.'

'You're right,' agreed Pastor Lotin. 'Last year, the Germans again blundered over the Moroccan question by sending their warships to Agadir to protect German interests there, while at the same time claiming the whole of French Congo.'

As well as more Kamerunian territory between the Logone and Chari,' continued Samba. 'This has only helped to fill the British, -the French, and the Belgians in the Congo with grave doubts about German scruples. In other words, Franco-British relations are even better than ever. And, given the interest they both have in our country, they wouldn't be averse to ganging up against Germany to oust her from here.'

'And when the Germans are gone?' the Pastor wanted to know.

Rudolph drummed on the table with his fingers, 'I say let's cross that bridge when we get to it. Our more immediate danger is Germany who has to be removed at all cost.'

'Which brings us to the next questions,' said Samba. 'Of whether a European war will come soon enough. I am almost willing to bet my right arm on the possibility of a war in Europe within the next eighteen months. How will this help us? With the Germans fighting a major war in Europe, we should be able, with French and British help, to give them a good beating over here.'

'And if there's no war?' Rudolph insisted.

'Then the job will be tougher of course. We can still count on France and Britain to help rid us of the Germans in any case, and that's the important thing for now.'

Zara had been having labour contractions all day without knowing it, so slight were the pains in comparison with what she had experienced with her first child. She was in her eighth month and did not suspect for a moment that her baby might arrive before another month was out. At midnight however, she woke up in a sweat and realised she was about to have the baby. As she tried to think what to do, another contraction coming fast on the heels of the last one sent her collapsing on the pillow with a howl of pain that rang through the whole house.

The three men conferring at the dining table looked questioningly at one another.

'Zara!' cried Rudolph, jumping out of his chair.

They reached her door just as a frightened Miriam was turning the knob to enter her mother's room.

'Kwedi!' Zara gasped when she saw them. 'Send for Kwedi.'

'My God!' Rudolph was aghast. Kwedi was in Deido. Could she be got there in time?

Zara collapsed once more with another scream. Samba made for the bed and drew off the bedclothes. The waters had already broken.

He turned to face the others, 'I'm afraid this might not be able to wait for Kwedi. Send somebody by all means but, we better be prepared to handle this ourselves.'

'Then I'll go and fetch Charlotte and Ma Bele' suggested Rudolph.

'No, No!' gasped Zara. 'Don't bother them. I'll be alright. Just send for' - she arched back again, in the throes of pain.

'You!' Samba pointed to Miriam. 'Get the others and set pots of water on the fire to boil. Quick!'

Miriam scurried out, dragging along with her Frederick and Alexan-der who had been watching from the door. The captain started rolling up his sleeves.

'Now Ndumbe,' Samba turned to Rudolph. 'You and Pastor set about getting things ready. I need two basins of clean water, some towels, a pair of scissors ... let's see, what else? Anyway, you two start getting those ready for me; I'll let you know as they occur to me.'

'Are you sure you can handle this?' asked Rudolph doubtfully.

'Like a breeze. I do it every day. Now clear out and let me get to work. And whatever you do, don't send for Charlotte and her mother.'

He waited until the two men had shut the door behind them before turning his attention once more to the woman on the bed. Pulling off the sheets again, Samba felt Zara's abdomen with his hands then lifted up her legs and bent to examine her. He straightened and covered her up once more. Wearing a confident smile on his face, he took her hand and squeezed it, then laid a soothing palm on her forehead.

When the pain gripped her anew, she clung to his hands in despera-tion but hardly made a sound.

'That's my brave girl,' Samba smoothed the sweat off her brow. 'Everything's going to be fine, just fine.'

Between two spasms she opened her eyes to find the deepset eyes directly above her face, staring down at her.

'My Lord,' she smiled up at him.

'Yes, my love?'

'I -I thought I had lost you.'

'You haven't lost me, Zara.'

'Don't go away again.'

'Never!'

Rudolph came in with a basin of water in his hands, towels thrown across his arms, to find the labouring Zara whispering with his friend. He put down the basin and hung the towels on the canopy.

'Shouldn't you be getting ready for the operation - Doctor?' he called on his way out again.

'All in good time, Ndumbe. All in good time. Has somebody gone for your wife yet?'

'The boys left half an hour ago.'

Pastor Lotin came in just as Zara let out another scream. Samba whipped off the bedclothes and bent down to examine her a second time.

'Goddamit, Rudolph, get the hot water in here right away. And where are the scissors I asked for?'

Rudolph dashed out as Miriam flew in.

'Is it coming?' demanded the girl excitedly.

'Yes,' replied Samba. 'And you'd better stay here and help me. When the hot water comes, mix some of it with enough cold water not to scald the baby's skin. And find some clothes for the damn baby. They must be in here somewhere.'

'Yes Sir!' Miriam set to work as soon as Rudolph came in with the water.

The woman on the bed started yelling non-stop.

'The baby's coming!' shouted Samba.

'Holy Jesus bless us,' the Pastor started praying.

Her eyes popping out of her head, Miriam stood by Samba and watched the birth of her baby brother. When Samba called for the scissors, she had it ready. Having severed the umbilical, she watched the captain hold the bloody infant upside down and give him a sharp slap on the behind that sent the baby yawling. Then it was placed in her arms with instructions for her to clean its nose and wash it while Samba, perspiration beading his face, turned once more to help the mother expel the afterbirth.

By the time Kwedi got home at five-thirty that morning, it was all over, Samba in his room, Zara and the new baby in theirs, the three of them fast asleep recuperating from the night's exertions.

It was a Sunday, but one filled with far greater celebration and merriment than usual. This was the day of the Ngondo when the Douala council of notables was convened to meet at chief Akwa's palace. On the second floor of the old chief's splendid two-storey residence, members of the council were gathered in an atmosphere of gravity that contrasted sharply with the carnival outside.

Rudolph was just ending a speech: '. . . My brothers and fathers, Martin-Paul Samba has been urging us for the past ten years to show the white man a united front.

For those of us who have been hesitating, the present crisis has pointed out the way for us. If we allow ourselves to be pushed out of our own land, we become less than captured slaves - it would be the beginning of what I see as the extermination of our race from the face of this earth.

Our country stands in peril - it is therefore no time to remember grudges. Let us put aside for the time being all our differences. Later, when the danger is over, when the enemy has left this country, each of us may once more take up his favourite quarrel where he left off. I will now call on Martin-Paul Samba, chief of Ebolowa - you all know him as the Captain. Chief Samba will now explain to you the strategy we propose to follow in this matter.'

Rudolph returned to his seat as Samba took the floor.

Later that same evening, the meeting over; Samba descended to the Akwa courtyard where a talented group of musicians kept the throng of merrymakers enthralled with a heady beat that had everybody on their feet. Making his way through the gyrating crowd, he bumped into Miriam dancing among a group of her teenage friends.

'Hello,' invited the girl. 'Won't you dance with me, Captain?'

Samba smilingly obliged her with a few steps of Makossa before asking. 'Is your mother here?'

Miriam clapped her hands in triumph, 'I knew it! I knew you'd ask!'

'Well, I just wondered, you know.'

She giggled at the captain's obvious discomfort, 'Oh, you should see your face! No, Mama decided to stay home with little Rudolph.'

'Must be lonely for her.'

'Oh, she's used to it.'

In another part of the courtyard, Charlotte-Amelia came dancing up to James Akaku. She was resplendent in a blue printed kaba ngondo of ample proportions, held to her slim waist by a leather sash. Her head was crowned with an intricately tied scarf of the same printed fabric. Big round bands of heavy gold earrings hung at her ear lobes, while both her wrists jangled with beads and bangles.

'You look like the legendary Adama, the princess of the Niger' Jim complimented her.

Charlotte-Amelia said nothing, merely dancing with the abandon of a person possessed. After a couple of minutes, she asked, 'What're you doing tonight, say in about two hours' time?'

'Nothing special,' answered Jim. 'Why?'

Charlotte-Amelia drew closer and said in his ear, 'I have a sugges-tion.'

'Yes?'

'Today's Ngondo and I have no panties on. Meet me at the turning on the path leading from our house to Ndedi's aunt's. You won't regret it.'

James Akaku grinned from ear to ear, 'I'll be there.'

As soon as he could escape, Samba set off for Rudolph's palace, Zara was on the back porch nursing her child. She had a welcoming smile for Samba as he came striding into the compound.

'Hello, Zara,'

'Hello, Martin-Paul.'

Samba drew up a stool and sat opposite her. For a moment he watched the infant sucking noisily at its mother breast.

'Now, this is one hungry young man!' Samba reached out a finger and tapped on the baby's cheek. 'Hey, slow down and say hello to your godfather!'

Little Rudolph went blithely on eating, curling his tiny fingers round Samba's giant forefinger. The two adults watching him laughed. Since the birth of Rudolph-Samba, a sense of attachment and complicity had drawn Zara and Samba closer to each other.

Samba removed his finger from the baby's grip. 'I'm going back to Ebolowa tomorrow. But before I leave. I want you to tell me something.'

Zara turned all her attention to him, 'What?'

'Whom do I remind you so much of?'

She continued looking into his eyes for a while before answering, 'My daughter's father.'

'Who's he, Zara?'

'He was a Zulu chief, a famous warrior like yourself. When I first saw you, I almost believed it was him come back to me from the dead.'

'Tell me about him, Zara/

Her eyes looked troubled, 'I don't want to recall his story now. It's too confusing for me at this moment. Your resemblance to him is very unsettling.' Her eyes were anxious almost as if pleading with him to help her resolve the mystery of his uncanny resemblance to her Zulu lover.

Samba turned away from her gaze to watch fascinated at the infant still sucking hungrily at Zara's bosom. Samba's eyes travelled slowly up to the round mound of her breast over to the pronounced cleavage separating it from the other breast. He did nothing but look at her but the woman before him felt as if he was slowly running a caressing finger up

119

and round her breast. The sensation produced by the suckling child suddenly acquired a sharper intensity that caused Zara to force the baby's lips away from her nipple with a cry as if she had been bitten. Little Rudolph howled angrily at being thus rudely cut off in the middle of his meal. Zara stood up and tried to calm the baby as well as herself, but her mind was in a turmoil.

Samba also rose to his feet. For a moment they faced each other like two prize fighting cocks ready to pounce on each other. Footsteps pounded on the hard floor of the compound. They both turned guiltily to see Rudolph approaching. For a moment the three of them stood in a circle while Rudolph looked from Zara to Samba and back again. Little Rudolph was still bawling his head off. Zara turned abruptly and entered the house. Alone in her room, she sat down trembling to finish nursing her baby.

Outside Rudolph asked Samba, 'What's up?'

'Nothing, as far as I can tell.'

They looked at each other challengingly.

'Listen,' Rudolph said finally. 'That's my cousin's wife, you know.'

'I know,' replied Samba.

Miriam hurrying home from school, ran into Frederick, Alexander and Jason-Kinge waiting for her at a road corner.

'Aren't you coming swimming with us today, Miriam?' they asked in a chorus.

'You fellows go on ahead. I'll meet you at the beach.'

'Hey, you never used to go home first. What's with you these days?' Kinge demanded.

'Mother hen, Mother hen!' Frederick and Alexander teased. 'She has to hurry home and suckle the baby before anything else.' They fell giggling into each other's arms and collapsed onto the grass, howling in mirth.

'Hey, Mbonga' Kinge feigned surprise. 'Didn't know you had sprouted oranges on your chest so soon. Let's take a peak.'

'Very funny,' Miriam told them disdainfully. 'Unfortunately, I don't have time to stand babbling with you children.'

'Mother hen! Mother hen!' they called as she hurried off.

At the house Miriam flung her school bag on the porch and ran into her mother's room. She snatched the little bundle from her mother's arms and moved towards the window. Four week-old Rudolph-Samba whimpered as his sister rubbed her face against his.

'He's angry at being disturbed.' his mother explained mildly. 'He was just falling asleep after his meal.'

'Was he? Oh, you lovely, Pretty!' his sister cooed. 'Don't be angry at me. I only wanted to say hello!' She gazed into his tiny screwed up face in enchantment. 'Didn't you miss me? Eh? Didn't you miss your sister? Here, don't cry. I'll let you go back to sleep.' She laid the small head on her shoulder and rubbed the baby's back until he dozed off again.

'I suppose now that you've found a job and a house you're going to send for your wife.' said Charlotte-Amelia. Her beautiful face was distorted with rage as she sat up in the bed. She seemed on the point of bursting in uncontrollable anger. Suddenly however, she gave a short amused laugh.

'Shit!' she exclaimed swinging her legs onto the cold floor, 'I'll be damned if I let her drive me away from you. Let her come. But I'm not staying away from you!'

'Isn't that going to be rather difficult?' asked Jim looking up at her from the bed.

'I don't know and I don't care. That's going to be your problem -keeping her in the dark about us. Not that it's going to be any use though. Sooner or later she is going to have to face the realities of African life, which they all seem to have forgotten since the white man carried them over there.'

'True, true,' agreed Jim staring thoughtfully at the mosquito net that hung suspended on poles over the bed.

'You should have known better than to go and get married to a foreigner' Charlotte-Amelia told him.

'I didn't want to, I had no intention to.' Jim said to the mosquito net.

'Then why did you?'

'You have no idea how persistent these American girls can be.' There was genuine regret in his voice. Charlotte-Amelia threw him a look of disgust and stalked off naked and angry to the bathroom. After a moment, Jim got up and followed her there.

Chapter Six

As 1911 dawned, Governor Otto Gleim, following instructions from Berlin, started making preparations for the expropriation of Douala land around the Wouri estuary. While this was going on, the Governor, who genuinely sympathised with the Kamerunians, tried to point out to his superiors the inadvisability of such an act. His protest of course fell on deaf ears. Secure in his military superiority, the German Kaiser saw no reason to worry about the discontentedness of his colonial subjects.

'. . .This time (the Governor wrote), we may be going too far, I have a feeling this proud people are going to fight tooth and nail to keep their land. Indeed we cannot accuse them of insubordination as your majesty suggests. They have given us ample proof of their pliability in the past. We have ousted them 'from their monopoly of trade with the interior despite official promises of non-interference on our part. For years now they have been paying the government taxes levied on them, even though we know they are at bottom bitterly opposed to this imposition.

It is my biggest fear that the present protests may become violent. In their fight against this latest colonial 'outrage,' the Douala people have chosen a young firebrand, their paramount chief, Rudolph Douala Manga Bell, to represent them. We have reason to suspect that he might be in contact with guerrilla elements. . .'

The German Government began wondering whose interests Gleim was actually representing. In January 1912, he was recalled to Germany after only one year of service.

He was replaced by Karl Ebermaier who started evicting the Douala people from their homes. Rudolph Manga Bell sent a formal telegram of complaint to the Reichstag and was removed from his post in the German Administration. Despite a general European outcry and widespread rioting in Douala, the Africans were moved to their new settlements.

The little caravan consisted of Rudolph's immediate family, Zara and her children, as well as Felix's parents and their children. They arrived at Ebolowa after an exhausting seven-day journey which had been slow due to the presence of the children and the old couple. James Akaku had offered to take them with him to Buea where he had friends who would willingly have put them up, but Rudolph had preferred to send them to Ebolowa. Samba lodged then in his large compound, putting Zara and her kids in the care of his mother. Kwedi and her children he assigned to his own sister Nadja, who shared the big house with him, while Charlotte-Amelia and her parents were given a cottage by themselves.

'They should be safe in Ebolowa,' Rudolph said to his friend that evening as they left for Biba, Samba's military camp. 'My people are too restive. In spite of my advice to them to remain calm, many of them tried to resist the eviction.'

'I can guess the results,' Samba responded.

Rudolph sighed, 'The Germans were not playing games.'

They trudged along in silence.

'The Council also decided to send a representative to Berlin, for what that's worth,' Rudolph broke the silence.

When Samba made no reply he added, 'We have also asked Sultan Njoya of Bamum for support.'

'That should produce some results. The European war I have been predicting seems on the verge of happening. My spies in the colonial government tell me that Germany is likely to have her hands full righting the war on two fronts against France and Russia. Of course the diplomats have their work cut out for them trying to avert disaster. But you may take the word of an old soldier who is keeping up closely with European politics - war is imminent in Europe.'

'The question is how we're going to be affected.'

'The Germans are going to face a third front here in Africa. The Belgian governor in Brazzaville as well as the British Consul in Lagos, have already promised to send us reinforcements whenever we're ready to take on the Germans. However, I'm biding my time and waiting for war to break out in Europe before I attack. That's why I'm insisting that you keep the Douala people in check. Let's not shed blood needlessly.'

Rudolph nodded gloomily. 'I suppose you know what you're doing. I hope to God your friends don't let us down at the last minute.'

They had now reached the edge of the training camp. Samba touched his friend's dejected shoulder comfortingly. 'This is a difficult time for all of us, Ndumbe. But, believe me, if there's one thing I know, it's that we must keep a cool head.'

They were accosted by a group of scout soldiers who led them into the camp, Rudolph was impressed in spite of himself. Samba's army was a small colony of young recruits culled from villages as far away as Mankon, Foumban and Garoua. The Douala chief gaped at what Samba euphemistically called his 'stash of arms.'

'The government itself cannot own a much bigger arsenal than this' Rudolph queried.

'Oh, they have one or two types of weapons we do not possess,' Samba replied modestly. 'But with help from Brazzaville and Lagos, this should be ample. It's a pity you're leaving, so early tomorrow. You could have watched us at drill.'

'I have to hurry back. I left a very restless bunch of people back home. But I should be here again before long.'

The following morning, Rudolph gone, Jason-Kmge, Alexander and Frederick came up to Samba as he was getting ready to leave for Biba.

'We're going with you,' they told him. 'We're old enough now.'

Samba tried to discourage them. 'Do your parents know about this?'

'Our Father would be the first to give us his blessing if he knew,' said fourteen year-old Frederick.

'I'm not so sure about that Fred,' demurred the captain. You're a bit underage.'

'Not so I,' came Jason-Kinge. 'And my parents are right here to give me their blessing.'

'I'm not too young either,' said Alexander. 'I'm fifteen, almost sixteen.'

Frederick became petulant, 'If you go, I go too,' he told his brother. 'Fourteen going on fifteen is just as good as fifteen going to sixteen. Besides you're the heir. If anyone should be kept away from the battlefield, it's you.'

'Oh year?' bristled the heir apparent. 'Let's just see how you're going to keep me away.'

Samba snapped his fingers, 'Right, everybody's going!' The boys raised a hurrah.

'But,' continued the captain. 'You all better say goodbye to your parents because it's more than likely you won't be seeing them again until this is all over. Once in you stay in. I won't tolerate any desertion. Still want to go?'

'Of course!' they chorused loftily.

'Then let's get moving. You've got fifteen minutes to get ready. Don't pack anything. The camp is well supplied.'

The boys made their goodbyes as brief as they could, allowing their parents no time for remonstrance. The 'refugees' from Douala all stood outside to see them off. Miriam, three year-old Rudolph-Samba by her side, stretched out a foot and tripped Frederick as he passed by her.

'What was the meaning of that?' asked the boy as he picked himself up from the dust.

'Just testing mettle, soldier,' replied Miriam.

Frederick was disgusted, 'Some girls ought to be butchered!'

'You'll take care of my boys.' Kwedi whispered to Samba.

Don't you worry. They'll come to no harm,' the captain reassured her.

She stood waving with misty eyes as her warriors set off.

Zara and Auntie Ekodi got on like a house on fire. The old lady loved to talk about her family and, before the year was out, her guest had learnt all there was to know about Martin-Paul, Katie, von Morgen and Sonia.

'Even as a boy his friends envied him his place in Massa Kurt's affections,' said Auntie Ekodi talking about her Son. 'But when he came back from Germany, the people *hated* him for what he did to them in the name of the German Government.'

They were fixing their mid-day meal. Zara sat on a low stool, the fufu mortar between her knees, pounding away while Auntie Ekodi transfer-red boiled yam from the pot to the mortar.

'How did you feel about what your son was doing, Auntie Ekodi?'

'What I thought hardly matters, but I'm glad for his sake that he finally turned against the Germans.'

Zara stopped her pounding for a moment to hitch her skirt up over her knees so as to get a firmer grip of the mortar.

She asked before starting to wield the pestle again, 'What happened to change him so drastically?'

'The same thing that has kept him from marrying - love.'

Zara paused with the pestle in mid-air, momentarily stupefied by the response to her question.

Auntie Ekodi, all the yam now transferred to the mortar, rinsed her hands in a bowl of water and sat up before launching into her story. She told Zara about Sonia von Morgen and how Samba had gone to live with the von Morgens.

'What happened was only natural, I suppose,' went on the old lady. 'The young man and the young girl fall in love with each other. They wanted to get married. The girl's father said he preferred to have the wedding take place here. So as my son had finished his studies and was already a lieutenant in the army, he returned home and started preparing to receive his bride. Martin-Paul came home and waited. One year passed, two years. His letters went unanswered. Your fufu will get cold.' Auntie Ekodi reminded Zara who had ceased pounding to follow the woman's story.

As she resumed her task Auntie Ekodi continued, 'Meanwhile Martin-Paul was acting crazier and crazier, spending all his time fighting first this then that tribe for the Germans and in the process, winning the bitter hatred of his countrymen.' Auntie Ekodi marked a pause to watch Zara's movements. 'Finally a letter came.' She told of the letter announcing Sonia's death and the circumstances surrounding it.

'I bet Martin-Paul went insane after that' Zara commented. Auntie Ekodi looked at the young woman for a long moment, 'You're right. We all went through a terrible period after that. I prefer not to talk about it, but after my son became calmer, he finally saw von Morgen for what he was and this truth helped to set him free. Free to cut off all ties with the Germans and even launch into a fight to get them out of Kamerun. Up till now that has been his only passion of life. But now. . ,'the old lady left her sentence unfinished.

'Now what,' prompted Zara stopping.

'You have re-awakened him,' replied Auntie Ekodi simply.

'I. . .?'

'Yes, you beautiful strange girl from I-don't-know-where. I am grateful to you. I thought my son had left his manhood in Germany. Thanks to you he lives again. It matters very little to me that you're already another man's wife. If it's you my son wants . . . And don't think I'm fooled. You try to avoid him, but I can see your longing for him is just as great as his for you.'

'Auntie Ekodi, please!' Zara was not at all pleased at the direction on conversation was taking. 'Did he tell you that?'

'He doesn't have to tell me. I'm his mother and I have eyes.'

Just then they heard Samba's voice calling from the front of the house. As soon as he reached the backyard, he bent down and hugged his mother.

'You devil!' crowed Auntie Ekodi. 'We were just talking about you!'

'Something smells good,' said Samba, his eyes on Zara.

Although her fufu was now ready, she still sat her skirt hitched above her knees, perspiration had plastered her light cotton blouse to her body, revealing every curve.

'Why don't you stay for lunch?' invited Samba's mother. 'We've made some okra soup to go with the fufu.'

Zara wet her hands in the bowl of water and started kneading the yam paste into a big ball.

Samba hadn't taken his eyes off her.

'I think I will,' he said in response to his mother's invitation. 'But I have to go into town immediately afterwards. Hello Zara.' 'Hello, Martin-Paul.' 'Finally got word from your husband.' 'Felix?' 'Where? What does he say?'

'You will have to tell us.' He held out a bundle of letters. 'All for you. From him of course. Must make interesting reading when they arrive in batches like this.'

Samba stooped down and looked into Zara's eyes. A bead of sweat was coursing down her chest. Samba brushed it off with his finger just before it plunged between her breasts.

He hadn't taken his eyes off her face, 'Where shall I put your letters?'

'On my bed please, Martin-Paul.'

Christmas that year passed quietly. Rev. Pastor Lotin Same, his black congregation gathered in a field outside the town of Douala, gave a fiery sermon that brought tears to the eyes of his listeners. But he succeeded in making his Christians understand that patience was to be the watchword among them.

'. . . Brothers and Sisters,' he reminded them. 'The Israelites in Egypt waited in patience for God's sign. And he did not fail them. God never fails those who wait for Him to show them the way. And I can promise you this: Yes God's time is almost at hand. A few more days, a few more months, what does it matter if in the end we overcome the Evil that has landed in our midst?'

'Our Moses is here. I have seen him with my own eyes. He has his rod ready in his hand. It won't be long before he waves it over that mighty sea to let us through and drown our enemies in its bloody tide.

Oh, what a bloody bath awaits them my countrymen! But beware of becoming impatient lest the Lord, in His holy anger, scatters us further afield like unplanted grain before the wind. Vengeance is mine saith the Lord. And to you, my people, I say, we shall be avenged, Amen.'

And the forest woods rocked and echoed as the congregation responded in one thunderous voice, 'AMEN.'

As the people made their way back past their former homes to the reservation the Germans had forced them into, the news spread like wildfire among them:

'Something is afoot.'

'The Reverend Pastor and Manga Bell have plans.'

'It won't be long now.'

'Let us wait and see.'

The new year, therefore, opened on an optimistic note.

For Charlotte-Amelia, 1914 broke like a stormy cloud leaving her sad and depressed. Proximity to Samba had re-awakened of all her old passion for him. She died a thousand deaths a day at each sign of Martin-Paul Samba's indifference. She was tempted to run back to Douala and join the rest of the people living in the reservations. She thought of going to join Jim Akaku in Buea where he had decided to wait out the crisis. She did not know what to do with herself. She had decided that on Christmas eve she would get Samba to a corner and finally declare her love for him. She had it all planned out. She would play her last card, tell him of the flame that had burned in her breast all these years only for him. She would tempt him with her flesh. She would lay aside her pride and openly declare her love.

But Samba did not spend Christmas with his family. The captain spent the entire holiday period with his men in Biba. Charlotte-Amelia felt defeated. On the morning of January 2nd her mother found her crying quietly but bitterly in her room and, with a mother's intuition, immediately diagnosed her daughter's grief. For a moment, Ma Bele felt blind rage at her daughter for wasting her life pining for a man who did not want her.

Keeping a firm grip on her temper however, the old lady east about in her mind for something unhurtful to say to her child. But the best she could come up with was, 'I don't see what's so special about Martin-Paul Samba that you cannot even look at another man. Except, of course, that James Akaku who's already married and who's just taking advantage of you.' As Charlotte-Amelia looked up surprised her mother went on, 'Oh yes, I know all about you and the American graduate. You may fool your father but you don't fool me.'

As Charlotte-Amelia continued to sob brokenly her mother forgot her good resolutions and lashed out at her daughter, 'Samba doesn't love you Charlotte. He never has and never will. What's more he would lead you a miserable life if you ever had the bad luck of becoming his wife. You haven't got what it takes to keep a man like him coming for more. Indeed we have this much grateful for - that he hasn't let himself be attracted by your looks. He could have made use of you and thrown you away like a used rag the way that American graduate is going to do when his wife gets here. Then where are you going to hide your head for shame?'

Charlotte-Amelia looked at her mother with angry eyes puffed from crying, 'Jim Akaku will do no such thing. And Martin-Paul would never have thrown me away. I would have clung to him and made him marry me.'

Her mother gave her a pitying look. 'You don't even know the kind of man you've fallen in love with. Some men can be forced to do things they never intended to do. Believe me, what Martin-Paul does not want to do, he does not do. Now get that into your head and stop wishing for the moon. Find yourself a nice uncomplicated man who will love you and appreciate what you have to offer him. That is, if it's not too late. This nonsense over Samba has gone on long enough.'

If eyes could kill, Charlotte-Amelia's eyes on her mother at that moment could have spat venom with a murderous intent.

'What do you mean by if it's not too late? All you can think of is marriage, marriage, marriage, as if that were the be all and end all. Well it's already too late for me. I hope that sets your mind at rest. I'm never going to marry, I don't want to, so leave me alone. Leave me alone!'

Pa Bele entered the room at a run. 'What's going on here? Eh Charlotte?' He went to his daughter's side. 'What is it child?'

'Oh Papa!' Charlotte-Amelia clung to her father sobbing.

'Have you and your mother been at it again?' He turned to his wife, 'Sissi, have you been bothering this child again? When is this bickering going to stop? When are the two of you going to learn to live together like mother and daughter?'

Auntie Ekodi couldn't stand the sight of Felix's sister mooning over her son.

'Such shameless hussies are a disgrace to womanhood,' pronounced the old lady heatedly. 'What man would be interested in a woman who throws herself at him in such an unladylike manner? That girl's mother ought to sit her down for a good talking-to. There's something wrong with her!'

'She's only in love, Auntie Ekodi.'

'Love, love.' Auntie Ekodi was exasperated. 'The white man has turned our society upside-down with that word. Listen, it's not a woman's place to love before she's loved. That's the way it was when we were growing up and, believe me, it made for a more tidy way of life.'

Zara couldn't restrain her laughter 'Oh Auntie, you'll kill me with the things you say. As if the poor girl can control the way she feels.'

'There you go again with this crazy idea that Love is a monster that cannot be held in check. When we Africans had only the word "Like" to describe such feelings there was no question about their being able to be turned on and off. But now it's "Love" and, oh dear me, we're all helpless before it. Of course That Girl can control her feelings if she wanted to. You're being quite successful at controlling yours, aren't you?' Samba's mother gave her a sly look.

Zara clamped her lips tightly shut.

'Dear, dear, look at that face!' Auntie Ekodi chuckled and touched

Zara's shoulder. 'Don't you worry. My son will win in the end.

Whatever Martin-Paul wants, Martin-Paul gets.'

'He didn't get his German girl.'

'All the more reason why he won't let you get away my child.

Chapter Seven

In the front room of the hut, now his home, Rudolph Manga Bell faced his night visitor. A short elderly man of stocky build, the visitor kept darting anxious eyes behind and around him.

'You say you're a houseboy for the Governor?'

'Yes, Your Highness. The former Governor, Otto Gleim, brought me here from Victoria where I had worked as a labourer on the palm plantation.'

'Your name?'

'Bernard Musi, Your Highness. I am a native of Bali up in Bamenda.'

'You say you have something of importance to say to me?'

The man took a deep breath before answering 'Yes, Your Highness. But I want you to realise that I have taken a big risk in coming to warn you like this. If my master even suspects that I have been . . . But your life is in danger and I am your brother . . .'

'Don't worry, my man. I understand, and we will make sure that this does not get out. Now, let's hear what you have to tell me.'

Bernard Musi glanced round the room then drew closer to his host before saying in a near-whisper. 'They have found out about your plans, Your Highness.'

'What do you mean?'

'A German trader arrived from Lagos yesterday. I heard him telling the Governor over lunch that he had learnt in Nigeria that the Douala natives are planning an uprising. And that the British army in Lagos has promised to help the Doualas throw the Germans out of Kamerun.'

Rudolph was shaken. He examined the face of his informant in the inadequate lamplight and asked, 'Your master was discussing such a sensitive subject in your presence?'

The Governor's servant grimaced. 'They were speaking in German, Your Highness. I have never let my employers know that I can understand their tongue. That way they have always talked freely in my presence.'

'And you've learnt things you were never supposed to know.' Rudolph moved to a chair and sat down heavily. 'What else did they say?'

'Well, the Governor, he got very red and told his friend that he was sure you were the one heading the rebellion and - and he said he would have you arrested. Then the man from Lagos said they should not arrest you immediately. He said they should find out who else was helping you in Kamerun and also arrest him. And then he said that they should make an example of you that will discourage any more Kamerunians from trying to revolt. That is all.'

The room was silent for a full minute. Then Rudolph got up and shook the servant's hand. He reached in his pocket and drew out two German marks for the man. 'Thank you Musi. You'd better leave now before anybody else sees you. And I shall forget I ever saw you. Agreed?'

The man nodded, 'Goodbye, Your Highness. He backed out of the hut and disappeared into the night.'

After Musi had left, Rudolph sank back onto his wooden chair and held his head in his hands, lost in thought. Fifteen minutes later, he brought pen and paper from a small corner cupboard and sat down to write. It was a brief note with neither heading nor conventional opening which read: 'The powers that be are on to our game. So far I am the only one under suspicion so avoid any contact and speed up action. I cannot take the risk of coming there myself. Everything is in your hands.'

Leaving the note unsigned, he put it into an envelope and went into the next room where his youngest brothers, twins, were sleeping on a mat.

He shook them awake. 'Get dressed and be ready to leave for Ebolowa immediately. I have an urgent letter that must be put into Samba's hands and no-one else's. I don't want you to be seen leaving in the morning.'

Rudolph waited in the room until they had dressed and packed one or two necessities. Then he gave the letter to the older twin.

'Keep away from the beaten track,' he told them. 'And do nothing to attract attention to yourselves. If anybody asks you, you are in no way related to me. Is that clear?'

He gave them some money and sent them on their way.

Rudolph-Samba was the first to see the twins arrive that evening. He ran forward to welcome them but half-way there, changed his mind and ran back to the house to inform his sister of their arrival. Miriam had already heard little Rudolph bellowing out the twins' names and bumped into her brother at the door. Kwedi and the rest of the family had also heard. They were pleased but surprised to see the boys.

'Is something wrong?' Kwedi demanded fearfully.

The boys explained their mission. The women looked at one another.

'Martin-Paul could come to town today, tomorrow or next week' said Auntie Ekodi. 'We cannot afford to keep this letter. So somebody will have to take the boys to him.'

'But we don't even know the way and none of us is allowed there.'

Charlotte-Amelia reminded them.

'Nonsense! This is an emergency. Zara, you'll take these children to Biba as soon as they've washed and had something to eat.' Samba's mother decreed.

'I take them *there*' Zara's eyes widened.

'You expect *me* to do it?' countered the old lady. 'Now let's not stand here wasting time debating. Kwedi, get those boys cleaned and fed and send them over to my place as soon as they're ready to leave.' Auntie Ekodi turned on her heel, bringing the conference to an end.

Zara followed her to the kitchen. 'Auntie Ekodi, I'm *not* taking those children and you know why.'

Samba's mother laughed. 'Really Zara, if I have chosen you to perform this mission it's only because you're the most reliable person around. I'm not sending you into my son's arms. He will set his own trap whenever he's ready. Believe me, he would hit the ceiling if he thought I was doing his chasing for him.'

With much misgiving but unwilling to make an issue of the matter before the entire family, Zara gave in and set off with the twins at dusk.

Although she did not know the way, the soldier in her was able to pick up the well-dissimulated trail leading to Samba's camp. Within two hours they were at the gates waiting for Samba to be informed of their arrival.

Half an hour later they were in Samba's personal quarters, a round cabin with a bedroom and a parlour. Zara looked curiously round the parlour where she sat on a wicker chair just inside the door. Beneath a bright lantern hanging from the ceiling, a book-laden table stood with stationery and various African *objets d'art*, vying with each other for space. The floor had been smothered over with cement and a giant animal skin rug lay on straw near the bedroom door. Samba's guitar, out of its case, had been thrown negligently on the rug. A single window protected by a wire mesh had a heavy beaded curtain rattling gently before it as outside breeze wafted into the room. A faint not-unpleasant musky smell hung in the air. The room held an atmosphere of ruggedness and warfare familiar to Zara from long-forgotten times. She leaned back in her seat and let her senses wallow in the nostalgia that suddenly engulfed her entire being.

Samba, who had remained outside for a minute to issue instructions to his orderlies, now entered his eyes alighting first on his female guest.

'I'm very surprised that you were able to find this place, Zara,' the captain said, looking sharply at her.

'Oh. . .'Zara waved her hand nonchalantly.

Samba let it go for the moment and turned his attention to the messengers from Douala. He read Rudolph's cryptic note twice, three times, with a deepening frown before looking up.

'Has anything strange happened lately?' he questioned the twins.

They shook their heads.

'The day Ndumbe sent you here with this note, did anything happen out of the ordinary? Did he receive a visit from the government people?'

The boys answered in the negative.

There was a knock on the door. Frederick, Alexander and Jason-Kinge came in saluting the captain as they entered. Zara stood up to embrace them and exclaim at the change military training had wrought on them.

'Miriam won't recognise any of you next time she sees you.'

Frederick grinned happily at that. 'How's she Auntie?'

'She misses you a lot,' replied Zara. 'But she's doing fine. She's also beginning to look quite different from the girl you knew.'

Unable to imagine Miriam looking anything but thin and awkward, the boys laughed at this.

'Right then, you three take Beybey and Eyidi to your quarters. I'm sure you have a lot to show them.'

The trainees snapped to attention. 'Yes, Captain!'

Zara sat digesting the contents of Rudolph's missive while Samba watched her.

She stood up and walked to the window. 'You'll have to act before they link him up with you.'

Samba agreed.

'Only, I wonder if the time is ripe,' she continued.

'The time is *almost* ripe,' Samba replied. 'At this point two things might happen. If we open fire on the Germans here, either the Imperial Government will decide that things are too uncertain in Europe for them to pay us much attention or, and this is what I am afraid of, they might decide to take a grand stand and show the world how they can punish those who cross them. In which case they could turn the full heat of their war machinery on us with crushing results, since we have nothing to count on but limited French and English detachments on the West African coast.'

Zara nodded. 'We have to find out exactly what has happened to alarm Ndumbe. To declare hostilities on our enemies now, when we could have waited for them to be preoccupied with war elsewhere, would be a serious mistake.'

'The problem is how to meet with Ndumbe and find out if we really cannot wait a little bit more.'

Zara frowned in thought. Then her face cleared. 'I know, I'll go. They would hardly suspect me of being involved in anything like this.'

Samba was about to protest, but then he remembered that this woman had been able to find her way to his secret barracks.

'Would you Zara? I agree you would be the best person to try to get in touch with Ndumbe. You seem to understand things. . . Only take care of yourself. Don't take any risks.'

'I won't. Your Highness.' Zara's smile was enigmatic. 'At the least sign of danger I shall become invisible.'

Samba began to sense a quality in Zara he had never suspected before. She who, for him, had stood for the epitome of beauty and woman-hood, was now taking on a newer dimension that threatened to throw him off balance. The unconscious condescension which had up till now coloured his thoughts of her was fast fading away to be replaced by something that could only be likened to respect verging on awe. Not that he had held her in any disrespect. To the contrary, he had almost placed her on a pedestal. Only now the esteem he felt creeping up on him was different from that which had existed before. He was beginning to see Zara as more than just a woman, with all the connotations that the term had always held for him. He examined her closely as she stood by the window hands on her hips her eyes faintly dancing in amusement.

'You're laughing at me, Zara.'

'Of course, Martin-Paul. You look as if you just stepped on a banana peel and fallen on your head!'

'How aptly you describe my feelings!'

He stepped closer and held her by the wrists. 'How did you find your way to this place, Zara?'

'I followed the trail, Martin-Paul.'

'But there's no trail. There isn't supposed to be one.' His eyes bore into hers.

She swallowed hard and looked away. 'Nevertheless there is, my Lord.'

Samba pressed his body against hers. 'Where did you learn to be a soldier? Tell me, Zara.'

Zara could not answer. Her voice seemed to have lost its way somewhere deep in her breast. Where was she? In Samba's cabin or Nguni's tent? Whose deep-set eyes were these boring into her soul? HOW old was she? Sixteen or twice sixteen? The well-known face drew closer and closer. She felt herself slipping . . . Just as Samba's lips touched hers, someone knocked on the door. The captain cursed roundly in German before barking for the intruder to step in.

Jason-Kinge came in saluting smartly. 'The twins are hardly able to stand on their feet, Captain. I came to find out if they are spending the night or leaving.'

Samba turned an enquiring look on Zara.

'Let the poor kids go to bed,' she said. 'I can go back alone.'

She would not accept Samba's invitation to spend the night, however. 'It would be best if I left at once. I'll start off for Douala early in the morning.'

Her tone told him she was not to be persuaded. And indeed, as Zara bade him goodbye at the barracks gates, he reminded himself that matters of greater importance than his love affair with her were at stake. Not only Rudolph's life but his own as well as those of the Douala people was in danger. Best to push Zara to the back of his mind for the time being. But when this whole thing was over, he promised himself, when it was all over. . .

Two weeks later Zara staggered into Samba's barracks, half dead from exhaustion. Dressed in a dirty torn black dress and matching headscarf she looked as if she had not eaten since the day she left the camp. Her feet were bare and blistered her eyes red from lack of sleep.

'I got to Douala a week ago and started back almost immediately,' she .told Samba in a hoarse breaking voice. 'The place is in an uproar. Ndumbe had been arrested.'

'No!'

Zara pressed her aching eyes shut and nodded. 'Several others have also been locked up. Some have been killed in prison others in clashes with the army. They say the Germans got information about the planned revolt and are picking up people they suspect might be the leaders. So far, although I cannot say for sure, it appears no links have been found between yourself and Ndumbe. They say the Governor is threatening to execute him.'

'Heavens!' Zara nodded once more. T turned right round and came back with the news.' She made drunkenly for the door. 'Kwedi must be told.'

Samba grabbed her by the wrist. 'You're going nowhere. I'll take care of that part myself.'

She did not resist as he led her into the bedroom and started undressing her, shouting to an orderly for a basin and water. Her clothes off, he wrapped a loincloth around

142

her and sat her on the bed while he went into the front room and poured a mugful of strong tea, spiked it with brandy and took it in to her. He held her in the crook of his arm and forced some of the potent brew between her chattering
teeth.

By now the water had arrived and, somewhat revived, Zara obeyed Samba's order for her to step into the steaming tub. After bathing her from head to toe in two basins of hot water, he laid her on the bed and gently massaged her body with pungent manyanga, a medicinal oil made from burnt kernel. By the time he was through with his ministrations, she had passed out.

He stood by the bed and contemplated the statuesque body breathing rhythmically in slumber. Samba drew the light coverlet over her. Kneeling by the bed, he pressed his lips tenderly on the gleaming forehead, his heart constricted by a strange foreboding.

Before retiring that night, Samba wrote two letters, one to the Belgian Governor in Brazzaville advising him to start moving in his troops. The other letter, addressed to the English Consul in Lagos, bore virtually the same message. In the morning, an agent was despatched with the letter for Brazzaville while Samba took the other one to Ebolowa himself. After seeing the letter safely in the hands of his agent, a rich Bamileke trader stationed in Ebolowa, he made his way to his home.

His worried family bombarded him with questions as soon as they saw him. Kwedi was frantic with anxiety. Since the night Zara had returned alone from Biba departing so mysteriously early the next morning, Rudolph's wife had neither slept nor eaten well. The strain showed in her thin face and tired eyes. When Samba asked the whole family to meet him in his mother's cottage, Kwedi broke down.

'No, no, Kwedi,' Samba reassured her. 'It's not that bad. Come on, be brave. I have something to say to all of you.'

143

Kwedi tried to dry her eyes with the edge of her kaba but the tears kept flowing. 'My blood has been shaking in my veins for the past two weeks. All day yesterday my eyelids were quivering as if they had caught a fever. I told Nadja I would soon be shedding tears.' She turned to Samba's sister. 'Didn't I tell you, Nadja? Didn't I?'

Nadja passed a comforting arm around the older woman's shoulders and walked her to Auntie Ekodi's parlour.

When Charlotte-Amelia had fetched her parents, Samba stood in their midst and addressed them! 'It's not as bad as you're all fearing.' He took Kwedi's hand in his. 'Ndumbe has been arrested.' Kwedi collapsed onto the floor as the rest of Samba's listeners exclaimed in consterna-tion. Auntie Ekodi hurried over to help her daughter with Kwedi while Charlotte-Amelia sat watching Samba in stony silence.

'I want you all to be strong,' went on the captain. 'There's going to be lighting very soon. You, of course, will not be involved. Your job will to give absolutely no information whatsoever concerning my activi-ties. If you are interrogated, I left Ebolowa for Yaounde a month ago and you're not expecting me back soon. Is that clear?'

Everybody nodded.

'In spite of your fears you, in particular, will have to pretend that you haven't heard the news I've just given you. This is of the utmost importance if Ndumbe is to be saved.'

'What's happened to my Mama?' Miriam wanted to know.

Samba gave them the facts, adding. 'She'll be coming to join you in a day or two. In case of any crisis. I want you all to place yourselves under her guidance. If it becomes necessary to contact me, she will know what to do.'

Chapter Eight

The rainy season of 1914 came with the news of an imminent world conflagration sparked off by the assassination of an Austro-Hungarian Archduke in Sarajevo, Bosnia. As far away from Europe as Tanganyika, Togoland and Kamerun, the enemies of Austria and her ally, Germany, launched an intense anti-Aryan campaign, branding Germany an enemy of Liberty, a world scourge against which all peoples of the earth were called upon to take up arms.

To the ears of those Africans under the German colonial yoke, this propaganda was sweet music. From his Grasslands Kingdom in Bamum, the inimitable Sultan Njoya sent more reinforcements down to Martin-Paul Samba.

The German Colonial Government in Kamerun became extremely brutal as they felt themselves surrounded by hostile natives. No European of non-German nationality was allowed into the country. Kamerunians were searched in the streets and their homes raided for arms. In his prison cell, Rudolph Manga Bell was tortured in not admitting that he had sent for foreign military aid as well as for reinforcements from Sultan Njoya. A small German force was sent up to Foumban to arrest the Sultan. On their way there, the soldiers received information from unsuspecting natives which led to the tracking of Njoya's troops to Ebolowa.

Meanwhile, English forces from Nigeria were already waiting in the wings on the Kamerun border for Samba's signal. Likewise to the south of Kamerun, Belgian forces were on the alert. It lacked only Samba's go-ahead for them to start marching in on the Germans.

On the night of the July 27th the day Germany declared war on Russia), the German Commandant in Ebolowa, von Hagen, led a raid on Samba's palace. Luckily, before soldiers had completely surrounded the compound, Zara was able to slip out unnoticed. Flattening herself on the ground behind a clump of trees, she lay and listened as the military men ransacked the buildings and herded the occupants into the courtyard. Her heart skipped two beats as she heard her son wailing for her. She dug her fingers into the ground where she lay and willed little Rudolph to hush. His cries soon ceased thanks, Zara knew, to Miriam who was all but a second mother to the child.

One by one the captives were questioned as to the whereabouts of Samba. As the hostages claimed not to know the answer to this question, the Commandant ordered his men to keep their rifles trained ill them.

'Once more,' he bellowed. 'At the risk of losing your lives, where is Samba?'

He was answered only by a wringing of hands and more wailing. Von Hagen marched up to Pa Bele and held his gun to the old man's temple.

'No, no!' Charlotte-Amelia ran over to the Commandant in supplication. 'Martin-Paul left home over a month ago for Yaounde. We haven't heard from him since.'

Von Hagen struck the girl on the forehead with his baton and she fell immobile to the ground.

As Ma Bele ran screaming to her daughter's side, the Commandant turned his attention once more to the petrified septuagenarian.

'Speak or he dies' hollered the white man.

Ma Bele kissed the German's feet. 'Have mercy. Don't kill my man, Martin-Paul has gone to Yaounde and that's the truth.'

'You lie, woman!' shouted von Hagen, and the gun went off spattering Pa Bele's brains on his wife's face and hands.

Felix's mother sank onto her daughter's prone body, her limbs (moving in spastic jerks. Von Hagen pulled her roughly to her feet and (pointed his smoking gun at the unconscious Charlotte-Amelia. 'For the very last time, where is Samba?'

'As I love my daughter, he is in Biba!' cried the distraught mother. 'Spare her kind sir. The man you want is in a camp somewhere in Biba.' She knelt and bowed in prayer, her body shielding Charlotte-Amelia from the menacing gun. 'Samba is in Biba, in Biba,' she sobbed rocking from side to side.

Von Hagen looked up as the rest of the hostages vehemently contradicted Ma Bele's words. As he smiled and barked out an order in German, Zara took off for Biba at a run.

Samba entered his cabin dusting his hands on his trousers. It was almost dawn.

'Well, everything is in place. If von Hagen returned to his barracks for more men, they might not even be on their way here yet. Even if they are, I shouldn't expect them before noon.'

Zara was sitting cross-legged on the rug drinking from a steaming mug. She had donned one of Samba's spare military outfits, having come to Biba only in the light cotton night-slip she had gone to bed in that night. She held out her cup of tea to Samba who took it and sank down gratefully by her side. He leaned his back against the wall imitating her.

'What's going to happen when they come?' asked Zara.

'We mow them down. They're too few to be of any threat to us. I've already sent word to our friends on the borders for them to start marching in. If they received my letters in time, von Hagen will not be able to get any help. I only wish I had a means of knowing what's happening in Douala at this moment.'

They sat in silence, thinking of Rudolph.

'If anything happens to Ndumbe,' Zara said quietly. 'I hope they leave Kwedi her sons.'

Samba looked at her downcast profile. 'You are sad, Zara.'

'Very sad. My heart is full of misgivings. The white man always wins in the end.'

'What a well of comfort you are!'

She shook her head, refusing to rise to his bantering tone. '1 wish I was wrong. But I've seen too much to even try to delude myself.'

When that day passed without any sign of von Hagen, Samba was baffled. After two days, he said to Zara:

I think von Hagen had been smarter than we believed, I am certain now that he has sent to headquarters for reinforcements. He has guessed, rightly, that he cannot face us with the meagre force he possesses here.'

'In that case shouldn't we be moving away from here?'

'I've been thinking of it,' Samba agreed. 'It will take us two days to be ready to move and they might be here by then.'

'Still, we can't just sit and wait to be slaughtered. Let's start moving southwards. We could meet up with the forces from Brazzaville.'

But just as they were ready to leave Biba, scouts returned to barracks with news that government troops were closing in on them. Columns of soldiers had been spied advancing on them from the directions of Yaounde, Sangmelima and Ambam. Samba could not retreat south-wards as had been planned. In fact, surrounded as he was on three sides, the only way left open for him was westwards towards Kribi. And, as Samba pointed out, to move in that direction would be like walking into the lion's den, the whole Kamerunian coast being heavily garrisoned.

Samba was perplexed, 'They couldn't have mobilised these many troops within the short space of time that has passed since von Hagen came looking for me in Ebolowa.'

'Impossible.' agreed Zara.

'From the size of these forces they must have been making prepara-tions for at least a month.'

'A month? Then that means. . .'

Samba nodded. 'They must have known about my activities. But how in Heaven's name?' He walked up and down his mind working furiously. After a few moments the captain sank heavily into a chair and buried his face in his hands with a cry of anguish as understanding suddenly dawned on him.

A frightened Zara fell to her knees before him and touched him. 'My Lord, what is it?'

He took her hands in his. 'They must have intercepted one or both of my letters to Lagos and Brazzaville.'

'Impossible!'

Samba nodded vigorously. 'That's the only explanation.'

'Then - that means the help we've been counting on won't be forthcoming?'

Samba did not answer. He sat staring with unseeing eyes at the wall as Zara buried her face in his lap with a sob.

Then she stood up swiftly. 'You must escape - alone!'

He shook his head, 'I've thought of it. It's not possible.'

'Of course it is! We'll keep them busy here in the belief that you're amongst us while you make a getaway.' She took his arm and tried to pull him to his feet, 'Come on, there's no time to waste!'

As he continued to sit, refusing to budge, she stepped back furious. 'What's the matter with you Martin-Paul Samba?'

He rose to his feet and held her by the shoulders. 'Zara, if those Germans get here and don't find me, every soul in this camp will be slaughtered.'

'They wouldn't do that!'

'Every single soul Zara, believe me. And to what end? The British and French help we've been counting so much on is not yet here. Maybe I made a fatal mistake. Maybe if

149

I had taken action as soon as I got Ndumbe's note, the help we need so much would have been here by now. However, the question now is, am I going to sacrifice the lives of a hundred or so young men just so I, Martin-Paul Samba, might live?' He shook his head once more. 'They put their trust in me. The least I can do is to stand by them to the end.'

'What end? You cannot be thinking of facing these many troops!' cried Zara.

'No, it would be madness. We don't stand a chance.'

'Then why don't you just go and let your men give themselves up peacefully without a fight?'

'That's just the point, Zara. They're coming for me and if I'm not here, it's death for those who have helped me escape. I know them only too well Zara. If a few score black lives will help drive home a point, what's that to them? No, there's only one way out.'

'What's that?'

'Give myself up.'

'To those wolves?' Zara was aghast.

Samba leaned against the table. 'If I thought for a moment that their blood would help our cause, I wouldn't hesitate to sacrifice these men. But I've already told you, help is not at hand, it would make no sense. I owe it to the mothers whose sons I took on trust to see that their children do not come to a meaningless end.'

'There must be another way out, there must!'

'I wish there were, my darling.'

Zara flung her arms round his neck and hugged him desperately. 'My Lord, don't give yourself up - they'll kill you.'

'I know Zara.' His arms encircled her waist. 'I've already accepted that. At this moment, I have only one regret.'

She looked at him. 'What?'

Samba took her face in his hands and traced its contours with both forefingers. 'That I shall never kiss those beautiful lips.'

He smiled as he said this and Zara realised that his mind was made up. This was the end. He was giving himself up, knowing what awaited him.

She asked only one question. 'How far away are the government forces?'

'They should be here by mid-day tomorrow.'

She looked at him steadily. 'Then we do have some time don't we?'

That night, after Samba had issued orders to his men concerning the following day's activities, he retired to his quarters and locked himself in with Zara.

There was no question of sleep for them. They lay on the rug in the parlour and loved and laughed and cried and tried not to think what the morning would bring. Zara told Samba of the young Katangan Kazi who was driven from her home, then captured by a mighty Zulu chief who taught her to love before being killed himself by slave raiders. Samba told Zara of the young ambitious son of an Ebolowa labourer who won favour with a German explorer and was taken to Germany, where he had the audacity to fall in love with his benefactor's blond, blue-eyed daughter. It was a night Samba would recall as he faced execution at the hands of his enemies. It was a night that would haunt Zara to her death-bed.

The next morning at 10 a.m., while England was declaring war on Germany, Samba shook hands with his officers for the last time, waved goodbye to his soldiers and went to meet von Hagen who was waiting for him inside the camp gates.

Zara stood with Frederick, Alexander and Jason-Kinge outside the captain's door, fighting back the tears she had not wanted Samba to see. Around her several young men were openly weeping. She drew the disconsolate heads of Rudolph's sons to her breast and watched as von Hagen's men secured Samba's hands behind him before marching him off.

Goodbye she said wordlessly. My loss is little compared to the loss of your people. There shall never be another man like you.

Two days later, news had reached Africa that France, Britain, Russia and Belgium were at war against Germany and Austria. Without waiting any longer for the go-ahead from Samba, British, Belgian and French colonial forces started advancing simultaneously on Kamerun from Lagos, the Congo, Chad, Gabon and Ubangi.

The panic-stricken Germans in Kamerun decided to make an example of the 'traitors' Samba and Manga Bell. In a hasty court martial the two friends were found guilty of treason and sentenced to death. On the morning of August 8th 1914, Rudolph Douala Manga Bell was executed by hanging in his home town, while Martin-Paul Samba faced a firing squad in Ebolowa.

Unable to receive any reinforcements, the Germans in Kamerun suffered defeat after defeat at the hands of their invaders until, by the end of that same year, the British had captured Douala. Victoria, and Buea. After this, German strong-holds fell in rapid succession into the hands of the allies. When the Fortress of Mora in the North finally surrendered in February 1916, the First World War, as far as Kamerun was concerned, came to an end.

The Germans were evacuated from the Protectorate and interned in Spanish Rio Muni. France and Britain divided the country up between themselves. Kamerun became Cameroon for the British and Cameroun for the French. A new colonial era had begun for the former German Protectorate.

The End